LILAC AND OLD GOLD

A ZEKE TRAYNOR MYSTERY

JEFF SIEBOLD

Book cover design and interior formatting by Tugboat Design

ISBN-13: 978-0-9979570-2-0
ISBN-10: 9979570-2-6

Dedicated to Karin, my strongest supporter
and my greatest love.

CHAPTER 1

Zeke Traynor answered his phone.

"We need you up here, old boy," said Clive Greene. "Midtown Atlanta. The action is about to start."

"Your timing is impeccable, as always," said Zeke. "I can be there tomorrow." Then, almost as an afterthought, he added, "What's up?"

"Protection and a blackmail exchange," said Clive. He sounded distracted. "Hold on for a quick moment."

The phone went silent. As an occasional operative for The Agency, Zeke was routinely employed for personal protection, counterintelligence and investigative work. Mostly, the clients were government agencies who coveted the level of deniability that Clive Greene and his Agency provided.

Zeke had been standing on a pier somewhere on the west coast of Florida, enjoying the September sunshine and getting ready for some offshore tarpon fishing when the phone in his pocket had buzzed. He'd looked at the caller ID before he pressed the green "answer" button.

Thirty-eight and fit, Zeke's longish hair tended toward a lighter blond color in the sunshine. His eyes were surprisingly blue, a slate-blue color that he'd inherited from his father. It contrasted well with his present deepwater tan.

Clive, on the other hand, was a picture of British aristocracy, tall and pale and immaculate. Zeke could picture him in the office, standing regally by the window with perfect posture, his formal clothing perfectly fitted.

"I'm back," said Clive. He quickly filled Zeke in on some of the details- their phone line was secure- and indicated that he would arrange transportation before Zeke reached the airport. "You'll be flying out of Tampa, then?"

"Yes. Will you be setting up an apartment for me?" asked Zeke.

"I'll have Sally get you the details. We'll have just a short time to get set up. See you tomorrow." The line went dead. That was four days ago.

* * *

The small man on the sidewalk, the assassin George, had plenty of opportunity to look around discretely. As he approached the campus coffeeshop he saw a blond man inside who was ordering at the counter; a younger man, thin, probably a student, sitting at a table wearing ear-buds and looking at his computer; and the barista, a small girl with dark hair and a black apron. But he wasn't looking for these people. The fellow he was supposed to meet was a dark, Hispanic-looking man with black hair and glasses, Alberto Cruz. The man was supposed to be carrying a blue and gray backpack and wearing khaki pants and black shoes. He wasn't visible in the coffee shop.

There was a steady stream of vehicular traffic, employees and students leaving the campus for the weekend. On the street in front of the coffee shop, all of the traffic was heading east toward the campus exit and then onto the Interstate ramps. Along the near side of the two-lane street was a row of parallel parking spaces, most occupied by vehicles also facing to the east.

George reviewed the possibilities and then his options. Perhaps his target was in the bathroom. Perhaps he hadn't arrived yet. Perhaps something had spooked him, and he'd left. Or, maybe he'd lost his nerve.

Stay away, catch a cab and be invisible was one option, and a good one if there were any cameras in the area. He was certain that there were, this being a college campus. Best to stay off their radar as much as possible.

Or he could buy a cup of coffee and maybe find out a bit more about what was happening from the girl behind the counter, the barista. With that option he'd have a reason to stay around for a few minutes, in case the dark man was running late.

And then he saw him, the dark man, up ahead on the wide sidewalk. He must have come from just inside the coffee shop. His hands were empty, and he was walking in a determined fashion away from George, angling toward the street and about to step off the curb to cross. Looking both ways first, he stepped out into the traffic lane.

The dark man hesitated as a blue open-bed pickup truck

drove past; he then took a quick step behind the truck and in front of a black sedan, crossing the street in the middle of the block.

There is one other option, George thought. He could do what he was hired to do. He glanced to his left and nodded slightly at a parked vehicle with dark tinted windows.

* * *

There had been three people in the coffee shop, including the barista, when the dark man first walked in. He was a thick, barrel-chested man with Hispanic features, wearing khaki pants and black dress shoes. He stood in the doorway and looked around for a moment. Over one shoulder he carried a blue and gray backpack.

The barista was cleaning some equipment behind the counter. The other two in the coffee shop were apparently patrons, sitting at separate tables. One was a student wearing ear-buds and watching something on a computer screen, and a second man, Zeke Traynor, was sipping coffee.

Apparently not seeing who or what he had expected, the dark man set his backpack on the table nearest the door and turned back toward the front window and waited.

That's not Cruz, thought Zeke. Then, *wow, avoid wearing black dress shoes with khakis,* he thought with a smile. He glanced at the barista for a moment and then back at his coffee.

As Zeke opened his tablet computer, a woman pulled the front door open and the dark man had to squeeze aside, making sort of a half turn to get out of her way in the aisle between the tables. She was remarkable looking, with thick brown hair pulled into a ponytail and large brown eyes. Her face was symmetrical, and as Zeke watched she looked over at him and broke into a fantastic, wide smile.

She was wearing tight, black leggings and low boots. The top of her leggings was covered by a bright yellow, tailored silk shirt that fell to her hips. The shirt was cut like a man's dress shirt, but without the tails. She looked around and then walked directly to Zeke's table.

"I'm Tracy," she said.

"Hi, Tracy," Zeke replied. He closed his tablet and looked at her. Her makeup was subtle, skillfully applied so as not to attract attention, to deemphasize her wide-set eyes and full lips.

Zeke knew that she was 29 years old and that her full name was Tracy Johnson. And he knew she carried a Glock 26 in her purse- a gun made mostly of a light polymer. It had a five and a half pound trigger pull and held ten 9-millimeter rounds plus one in the chamber. But they weren't hollow point rounds; government agents don't load hollow point bullets. Hollow points leave ugly wounds, and there's too much risk of media criticism in the event of a shooting.

And, Zeke knew that Tracy worked for the Feds. More precisely, he knew that she worked for the Secret Service. Alberto Cruz had told Zeke all about Tracy. He wasn't surprised that she was there in the coffee shop for the exchange.

"I know this sounds crazy," she said, "but I've lost my dog, and I'm searching all the shops and stores around here to see if anyone has seen her. She's a Labra doodle, about 35 pounds..."

Zeke was already shaking his head. "No, haven't seen any stray dogs today..." he started. He also knew that Tracy was allergic to dog hair.

"...and has sort of yellow, curly hair. Oh, you haven't? I'm asking everyone," she continued, already looking around the room for someone else to query. "Are you from around here?" she continued.

"I live just over there," Zeke waved in the general direction of the front of the coffee shop. Tracy looked that way and nodded.

"But," he said. He looked at her eyes, playfully, until she felt the silence and looked back, returning his gaze.

"Yes?"

"Leave me your phone number, and I'll call you if I see your dog."

She hesitated, and then gave him an impulsive smile. "I'll do that," she said. "Be sure to call."

Tracy jotted her name and number on Zeke's coffee receipt, handed it to him and headed to the other occupied table.

When Zeke looked again, the dark man was moving. The backpack was still on the table, but its owner with the black dress shoes was walking out the door. *He can't be going for long*, thought Zeke; *he left the backpack*. But the dark man didn't slow after he was out the door. Instead he turned right, east, with some speed and kept on walking with a purpose. In a moment, he was out of Zeke's sight.

CHAPTER 2

Zeke jumped up and grabbed the backpack as he stepped out of the coffee shop into the cool air. He turned right, semi-jogging to close the distance between himself and the dark man. He spotted the black shoes and khakis as they left the curb, and then they paused and stepped behind a blue pickup truck. They were heading away from Zeke, at an angle across the street.

Zeke passed a small man who was standing on the sidewalk near one of the coffee shop's outdoor tables. He was about five feet tall and was looking away from Zeke, tracking the dark man crossing the street. As Zeke passed him on the sidewalk, the small man turned and looked past Zeke and nodded slightly. He had the stature of a student, but the face of a mature man. Then his eyes returned to Zeke's face, focused, appraising. He never blinked. The absolute focus and the force of the small man's gaze gave Zeke a sudden icy feel. *Like an emotional thermocline,* thought Zeke as he passed the man.

Zeke hurried along. His direction vectored him at an angle of interception that would cross the street while gaining on the dark man. He glanced left as he stepped into the street and started to call out at the same time. Almost silently, a yellow SUV – a late model Cadillac Escalade – whipped out into traffic and passed in front of him. Zeke felt the breeze and power of the accelerating vehicle, and it forced him to step back up on the curb.

The Escalade entered the lane at a run and, without slowing, smashed into the rear of a black Honda sedan while the dark man was between it and the blue pickup truck. The impact was loud and felt powerful to Zeke. The dark man screamed in pain. The Cadillac had tinted windows and no license tag, and it continued to push and grind mercilessly against the rear bumper of the Honda. The dark man continued to scream as he fell backwards, his knees shattered.

The dark man's legs were smashed, trapped between the Honda and the pickup truck's rear bumper. He was lying back in obvious pain, his head on the hood of the car and facing the sky but seeing nothing. He flailed his arms beside his head. Each push of the Cadillac further crushed bones and flesh, and Zeke could see that the man's knees were bloody and twisted at awkward angles.

Suddenly, the Cadillac driver reversed his direction, creating just enough clearance to steer left into the empty oncoming lane around the sedan and the truck. As he passed the Honda, the SUV stopped abruptly, and the passenger-side window dropped. Two silent shots hit the dark man collapsed on the hood, each one making his head jump. He jerked and lay still. Then the driver accelerated around the truck, turned right at the next corner and was gone. The incident had taken less than thirty seconds, and what was left in the street were the two black dress shoes and a river of blood.

* * *

Tracy was talking quietly on her phone and looking out the window as it happened. She heard the crash from the impact of the Cadillac and the Honda, and she heard the screams and the continued revving acceleration of the SUV's engine. She left the building and recognized the victim almost immediately. It was the same man that had stepped aside as she entered the coffeeshop minutes before. She hung up and dialed 911.

Most witnesses were frozen in place. Nearby drivers stopped their cars and grabbed at their cell phones. Pedestrians were processing the scene, but most seemed to have no good idea of what to do. The action in the previous half-minute was too horrific to understand, too violent to react to, yet too intentional to misunderstand. People began backing up, moving, turning away, as if distance might insulate them from the horror of what they had just witnessed.

Zeke moved quickly toward the accident and made his way to a point where he could see the victim. The two bullet holes in the dark man's head confirmed to Zeke that he was dead. The man lay silent and motionless. His brown eyes stared blankly at the sky.

Zeke moved back to the sidewalk, and as passersby began to talk with each other about what they had seen, he calmly walked the short distance to the corner and turned south on Cherry Street toward his apartment.

* * *

That escalated quickly, Zeke thought. He went over the events of the past ten minutes in his mind as he walked back toward his apartment. He'd arrived at the coffee shop thirty minutes early and enjoyed a cup of coffee while waiting for Alberto Cruz to arrive with the backpack. His job had been to protect Cruz.

Zeke Traynor had the wiry look of a snowboarder or a wrestler (which he had been in High School), and the easy smile that comes with self-confidence. At just a bit more than five foot ten, he was still in great shape, and he wore his blond hair a little bit longer than was currently stylish. His slate blue eyes were a gift from his father, and his economical movements were the result of his training.

While waiting in the coffee shop earlier, he'd finished his first cup of coffee, smiled at the young barista and pointed at his empty cup. She nodded and Zeke jumped up, grabbing the cup as he strode to the counter. He'd never really gotten into the "Tall, Venti" lingo, but the coffee was good, and the atmosphere was pleasant enough this Friday afternoon.

"Tell me your name," Zeke said to the barista, as he waited for the refill.

"I'm Susan." She handed back his full coffee cup. The fragrance from the coffee was a floral enzymatic odor, and Zeke found it very pleasant.

"I don't think I've seen you in here before." Her glance stayed on his eyes a half second longer than normal, but that happened to him fairly often.

"No, I'm new to this area, Susan. I just moved in down the street." He looked out the window and could see the Enclave in the distance, a transit-oriented high-rise of new loft apartments, its corner just visible from the coffee shop. He looked back at Susan. She was a thin girl with jet-black hair and pale skin. Not unattractive, but preoccupied serving coffee at this moment. "Call me Zeke," he said. She was ringing up his refill.

Truth be known, Zeke had moved into the loft apartment for its location, near Georgia Tech and Olympic Park, and central to Midtown Atlanta. The physical move was fairly straightforward, since he'd rented all of his furniture, and brought only a few essentials, including a couple of good books on his tablet. Zeke most always travelled light.

Wearing casual jeans and a polo shirt, Zeke looked younger than his 38 years. Susan was shorter than Zeke by several inches, but she had a long, thin look and a pleasant face. Her black hair was tied back in a ponytail.

"Great coffee," Zeke said to her. *Caffeine is great,* he thought, *but the polyphenols are miraculous.* "You know, this stuff gets better and better the more research they do." He looked around the shop. "It has antioxidant phytochemicals in it that do all kinds of cool things," he said to no one in particular. *Makes it a deal at two dollars a cup*, he thought.

Susan handed Zeke his receipt, and said, "Have a nice day."

He smiled without showing any teeth, and returned to his table.

It was then that the dark man had arrived.

CHAPTER 3

So, where did the blond fellow go who took the backpack? George had seen him leave the coffee shop with a backpack that matched the description of the one he was to take from the dark man, and make his way past him toward the corner. After watching the accident, George ran to the corner and saw him in the distance. He followed the blond man for a few blocks and watched as he used a key to gain access to an apartment complex through a side exit door. He still had the bag slung over his shoulder, and he was carrying a tablet computer.

George was a professional. That's why he'd been hired for this exchange. That, his relationship with his employer Jefe, the head of the cartel, and his knowledge about Alberto Cruz. George blended well and took pride in his logistical skills and awareness. Waiting for the blond fellow to re-emerge from the apartments, George had backed across the street and taken a position that allowed him to see the entrances on two sides of the building. A third side was an alley, and the fourth was the rear, or north side of the building. If the blond fellow exited to the north, there was still a good chance that George would see him, once he'd walked a couple hundred feet away from the apartment building. To the north, the road widened and then the campus opened up into a tree-lined grassy area, a commons, which provided a better line of sight than the areas near the buildings.

At the best vantage point George stepped into a restaurant, asked the hostess for a menu, and turned toward the large front window, facing north, as he appeared to study the food offerings. After a few minutes, he ordered a grilled cheese sandwich to go and insisted on paying for it in advance. It was $4.75 and he gave the girl a five-dollar bill and a one-dollar bill. "Keep the change," he said.

There was no doubt in George's mind that he would find the blond man, and more importantly, the backpack again. This exchange had a finite area, and the blond fellow had used a key to access the apartments. That meant he lived there or he knew someone who did. It meant that he'd be back, and would possibly walk back to the coffee shop once he found out what he had in the bag. Considering the linkages associated with the campus, the location of the retail establishments and classrooms, the layout of the campus, the public transportation access points and the seriously restricted parking availability, George calculated that there was about a 70% chance that he would see the blond man again, from this spot, and within the next sixty minutes.

* * *

Tracy hated being on hold. She always felt that it undermined her momentum. While waiting for her supervisor to answer, she walked down the street, first right, then left, backtracking and hoping for a glimpse of anyone with the blue and gray backpack. The accident victim hadn't had it with him, so she assumed that the blond guy, Zeke, had taken it.

There were people on the sidewalk, but mostly in small groups of two or three, and none that looked like Zeke. The backpack containing the money and the counterfeit printer plates was gone.

Dealing with the local Police Department had slowed Tracy down. Fortunately, she was inside the coffee shop at the time of the accident and was able to pacify the police with her ID and badge and a promise to call the precinct with a statement and come in for an interview, if necessary.

"Fitch," she heard from her phone.

"Boss, this is Tracy. We've got a problem. Cruz never showed. I think he sent someone, a messenger. The delivery was half done, and then the backpack disappeared. It looks like it was taken by a local on his way out of the shop, and the messenger was killed in a hit and run..."

"Wait, what?" said Fitch. "What about the pick-up guy?"

"Haven't seen him yet, unless it was the guy who took the bag. But I don't think it was. It's a circus here." Tracy had turned the corner and walked most of a block. Now she was moving back toward the coffee shop entrance, avoiding the recently applied police tape and the uniformed officer guarding the scene.

"Where are your spotters?" Fitch asked.

"In place in the building across the street," Tracy confirmed. "This was supposed to be a quick and easy one."

"What spooked Cruz?" asked Fitch. "He knew he was covered."

"Not sure. Maybe he worked himself up to it. I'm circling the block, and I'll check in with our guys." She hung up and dialed the number of one of the Secret Service agents across the street.

CHAPTER 4

Zeke's apartment was in a mid-rise, urban style building with a brick and stone facade and black wrought iron trim on the balconies. The complex was maybe four blocks away from the campus in the trendy Luckie Marietta District. It was one of the newest apartments in the area, built a couple of years ago on the site of a former freight warehouse.

One benefit of living on the third floor, thought Zeke, *is that it's a short climb up the stairs.* He took them two at a time, then crossed the third floor mezzanine in four normal strides. He noticed that the 'tell', a small piece of clear plastic wedged between the door and the frame, was undisturbed. Zeke was in his apartment a moment later.

As soon as the apartment door was closed, Zeke bolted the lock. It felt like it might help keep the ugliness of the past few minutes separated from him, separated from his reality. Then he set the backpack on his kitchen counter and zipped it open.

* * *

Whatever was inside the backpack was wrapped very tightly in some sort of green plastic wrap. It was the kind of thick wrap that manufacturers use to keep their products together and tight during shipping. The first package was translucent, and about the size and shape of a large book or a thin laptop. Zeke lifted it out and examined both sides for an access point. There was none. It looked as if the wrap had been heat sealed to create an integral seam.

That's odd, he thought.

Zeke opened the drawer to his left and took out a pair of kitchen scissors. As he worked he smelled an inky smell. He'd picked up a tune in the coffee shop—a piano piece. Without realizing it he found himself snipping the wrap in time to the music still in his head.

The package began to come apart, and Zeke used both hands to contain the contents. That proved to be inadequate, though, as banded bundles of what looked like U.S. currency tumbled free, some bouncing on the counter, some into the sink, and much of it falling onto the floor. Zeke saw $100 bills everywhere.

He leaned forward and pushed the bundles he held between his chest and his hands onto the counter, and then reached down and began picking up the stacks from the floor. Each stack was marked with handwritten initials and a "$5,000" printed on the band wrapping the bills. Zeke flipped through two bundles and counted fifty one-hundreds per bundle.

Zeke stacked the bundles on the counter and counted them. There were forty-two perfect bundles of United States $100 dollar bills. He noticed that they'd been arranged in a shape that resembled a laptop computer, a rectangular shape, and three stacks wide. The green plastic wrap littered the floor in two pieces, and the backpack had fallen into the sink with a small thud.

Zeke looked in the bottom of the backpack. There were two cloth bags in the bottom, with drawstrings at the top. He pulled one open. It contained a metal printing plate that looked long and rounded on one side, with the reverse image of what looked like U.S. currency.

"Well, take a look at this," Zeke said to no one in particular, thinking about the connection between the guy with the Black Dress Shoes, the money, the printing plates and the accident. And then he heard a knock at his door.

CHAPTER 5

Instinctively, Zeke turned and opened the freezer door behind him, and started tossing the bundles of currency inside. Then he picked up the two pieces of green wrap and threw them on top of the money. And finally, he put the cloth bags back into the backpack, folded it once and shoved it on top of the pile. He shut the freezer door. There was also a small cardboard spacer, a block used to square off the bundles of cash, which he dropped in the trashcan as he turned toward the apartment door. Zeke's instinct was that he was probably followed from the campus.

Then came the second knock, a bit louder and more insistent. It wasn't official, as no one was yelling through the door at him, but the sound was coincidental and seemed a bit odd. Zeke walked quietly toward the door. Typically, Zeke avoided peepholes. A darkening lens is a sure give away of the position of the viewer's body and head, and a simple gunshot through the door, at the moment the lens darkens, has a good chance of hitting flesh.

Zeke had installed a small camera in the outside hallway to the left of his front door. It was mounted ceiling height and connected by Wi-Fi with a small monitor, a pad really, that was kept in an open cupboard in the hallway. He glanced at the pad and saw a small, dark haired woman smiling up at him. *It's Kimmy,* he thought.

Kimmy was a neighbor, a single woman who had introduced herself to Zeke the day he'd moved into the complex. She lived across the hall from Zeke. Based on the positioning of their apartments, her porch must have had a view north, down the street toward the Tech campus.

Although Zeke had lived in the Enclave for three days, it seemed as if he had run into Kimmy at least once each day. She was usually at the mailboxes when he stopped by, and she caught him in the hall often. She frequently knocked to ask for his assistance with any one of a myriad of small things, none of which she seemed able to handle by herself. She was a bit odd in that she seemed to embrace the spiritual world, and often went on about energy fields and the battle between good and evil. A bit nutty for Zeke's taste, but she could be entertaining.

Zeke opened the door a crack, as Kimmy lifted her arm to knock again. "Hey, Kimmy," Zeke said. "I'm sort of in the middle of something…" he started.

"Do you have a girl in there?" Kimmy asked with a smile. Kimmy was a body in motion, always moving, bouncing, turning; she was energy finding reasons to stay moving. Combined with the smile, the constant motion seemed to give her an attractive and young presence.

The comment made Zeke pause. He looked at Kimmy for a moment, and said, "No. But..."

"Good, I need to talk with you, Zeke." She walked past him into the apartment. As she passed him, Zeke smelled a hint of lilac. It was her usual fragrance and smelled fruity and ethereal. Kimmy rounded the kitchen island, boosted herself up on a stool and put her elbows on the granite counter. She was just over five feet three inches tall, with a round face and dark, curly hair. She had almond shaped eyes, the shape enhanced by subtly applied eyeliner, and her normal expression included a wide smile. It seemed that she was always moving, always smiling, and she had an optimistic yet practical disposition. Kimmy was dressed in a turquoise blouse, silver jewelry and a long Indian skirt. Although Zeke guessed that she was in her late 30's, from a distance she looked as if she were 25 or even younger.

Zeke followed her into the kitchen and glanced at the fridge for a moment, confirming that the door was still closed. He turned back to his visitor. "Sure, Kimmy, how can I help?"

"I saw you coming back from campus," she said. "Did you have a late meeting or something?"

"No, I stopped for a cup of coffee after my last class. I was..."

"How about a glass of wine?" Kimmy jumped down from the stool, opened the wine fridge and grabbed a bottle from the bottom shelf. She took a clean glass out of the cupboard, twisted out the cork and began to pour herself some Merlot.

"Would you like one?" she asked.

There are a lot of good arguments for red wine, thought Zeke, automatically. *The resveratrol protects against dementia and enhances cardiovascular strength. It's also responsible for longevity. The quercetin kills cancer cells, and the tannins contain procyanidins that protect against heart disease. But, not just now,* he thought.

"No, just water for me," Zeke said, taking a cup and filling it from the tap.

"I need some ice," she said, and stepped to the fridge. Zeke stopped breathing for a moment, but Kimmy pushed her glass against the ice dispenser in the fridge door, and three cubes slid out into her glass.

"Did you see the accident?" Kimmy asked. She corked the bottle, put it back in the fridge, circled the bar and hopped back up on the stool with her wine glass in hand. "The hit and run?"

"Is it on TV already?" asked Zeke. "I was there and saw it from a distance, but it only happened a few minutes ago..."

"A friend texted and told me about it. I guess word is spreading across the campus."

"It was awful," Zeke said. "The guy was just crossing the street. A horrible accident."

"Oh, no," Kimmy shook her head. "That wasn't an accident. When something like that happens, evil is always nearby and involved."

She said it with absolute certainty with no smile on her lips. Then she smiled broadly again, winked and sipped her wine.

"You think?" asked Zeke, not certain whether she was serious or joking.

"Sure," she said. "Did you ever notice how the universe likes balance? It actually seeks equilibrium. If it were random, things would just occur in equal number, good and bad, right? But the world is fundamentally good."

"Maybe I'll have that glass of wine, now," Zeke said, smiling at Kimmy.

"No really, think about it. The real 'bad' things that we see are isolated incidents that disturb the equilibrium. There's a greater evil that's at work, but it's limited by the good."

"Well, what can I do for you, Kimmy?" said Zeke, changing the direction of the conversation. Kimmy had once told Zeke about a family of gypsies that lived in the desert near her parents' house in Israel where she'd grown up. Apparently, they would play tricks on the local people and then return to their camp and laugh hysterically. Kimmy said that sometimes at night she felt like she was the only one who could hear their laughter.

Kimmy's father had been a banker in a rural town near the West Bank, a widower who raised his only daughter after his wife died in a market bombing some years before. Kimmy had fine, fragile looking features, and had told Zeke that her looks favored her mother. There was a picture of her parents on one wall in her apartment, and Zeke had acknowledged the resemblance.

"I should wait to ask you for your help until all this is over. It's really not that important, Zeke. I just need some help moving some furniture." She smiled again, looked at him with her big, brown eyes, and slid off the barstool. She set her empty glass in the drain and walked to the door, turned the knob and let herself out.

"Ciao," she said, and winked at him.

Zeke waited a moment after Kimmy left, and then he moved to the door and snicked the deadbolt. He returned to the kitchen, reached into the freezer and pulled out the chilled bundles of money, the plastic wrap and the backpack.

Zeke set the backpack on the counter and took the two smaller bags with the drawstrings out of it. Opening the top of each carefully, slowly, he saw they both contained the same thing, a curved counterfeit printing plate. The plates were solid and substantial, each individually wrapped in a thick cloth and held in place with industrial strength rubber bands. Zeke didn't notice any ink stains or smudged area on the cloth, but he had smelled ink, so he assumed that these plates had been used but cleaned.

He unwrapped each plate carefully. There were four reverse images of the front of $100 bills, and four reverse images of the back of $100 bills. They had heft, maybe fifteen pounds each. A newer Simultan printing press with a few of these plates could produce 10,000 sheets of new money an hour.

He arranged it all on the countertop and noted the time.

It was 5:37 on the microwave clock.

Chapter 6

As he long-pressed the off button to reboot his phone, Zeke thought about the evil that Kimmy had mentioned. It could be true. He remembered the feeling as he had passed the small man on the street. *Like a sudden thermocline, a tangible temperature shift.*

The small man could have been involved, thought Zeke. He'd looked past Zeke first, and had given a small nod toward someone behind Zeke, possibly someone on the sidewalk, or even in a car. The gesture had looked to be affirmative, a command.

He looked at the pile of money in front of him. *U.S. Currency,* Zeke thought. But these bills were the older, pre-2013 $100 bills. Before the holograms and special threads had been added. This currency was one version behind current.

Zeke checked the serial numbers on the $100 bills. They were all the same four numbers, all counterfeit. So, this was a package of sophisticated counterfeiting equipment and product. What seemed most unusual was that Black Dress Shoes had walked away from it all.

There was nothing else in the pouch, so Zeke emptied the cash and the printing plates into his brown leather backpack, plugged his tablet in a wall outlet, threw his backpack over his shoulder on one strap, and walked out. By now Tracy would have figured out about the backpack. She'd be looking for him.

Using a different stairwell, Zeke exited a side door and turned the first corner north toward the Tech campus. Almost immediately he blended in with the student and pedestrian traffic.

* * *

Minutes later, the small man, George, spotted the blond man walking north from the apartment complex. He was carrying a leather backpack, which he had slung over his shoulder. He was about 150 yards away and walking away from George. *Perfect,* George thought, and he immediately left the restaurant without his to-go order. He walked quickly.

George was steadily gaining on the blond man, and was about twenty yards back when he slowed and paced himself. From behind, George saw a slim, fit man with an easy, balanced walk that spoke of competence and conditioning. A few people have that natural, genetic muscle motion that translates into excellent balance and quick reactions. This fellow seemed to be one of them. And he appeared to be heading toward the library building, walking comfortably.

George watched the blond man approach the main entrance of the library at the same time as two college-aged girls, and he held the door open for them. He used the opportunity to check behind and around him, carefully. Across the open area of the campus there were people walking in almost every direction, some hurrying along, some talking as they walked together, several looking down at their phones as they walked more slowly. Apparently, nothing stood out, and the blond man followed the girls into the lobby.

* * *

Zeke was in the campus library, having used his student ID to gain legitimate access. The leather backpack hanging on the back of his chair blended in well and seemed to reinforce his student status.

Although he was actually on assignment here, posing as a student gave him freedom of movement and flexibility. He took out his encrypted cell phone.

"Clive, here." He heard the familiar voice with a touch of Aristocratic England in the rich baritone.

"It's Zeke. Most curious, I was at the exchange, the coffee shop, and a fellow showed up with a backpack, hung around for a few minutes, then left the bag on a table and took off. He didn't get across the street before he was neutralized. It looked like a pro hit."

"And the bag?" asked Clive.

"I have it. I'm planning to get it somewhere safe and hidden quickly," said Zeke.

"Do you require assistance?" asked Clive.

Zeke smiled. "Not yet," he said, and hung up the cell phone.

First order of business, he thought, *is to get this bag someplace safe.* He pulled a random book from a nearby shelf, sat and pretended to peruse it.

Earlier, while walking, he had planned for safe interim storage. Eventually, he would arrange for someone in The Agency to pick it up and get it back to the Secret Service.

It's too awkward to mail or ship it to myself, he'd considered. *And it's too big to hide it easily.* There were people he could have asked to hold it for him – in the office at the apartments or maybe a librarian – but that involved other people, and other people were an additional risk. In the meantime, he needed it safe.

The campus Student Union had lockers for rent, the kind you could find in an airport or bus station in some places. You could put your item in the locker, push in a couple of dollars in quarters, and extract the key for short-term storage. Not a bad option, and pretty anonymous with no trail leading back to Zeke if it were found.

Looking around the library, he noticed the same people as when he entered the room—no new faces. He settled in to read for a reasonable amount of time before heading across campus to the Student Union. If anyone were following him, he'd wait for them to show themselves.

Zeke selected the local paper, as well as a copy of *The Economist* magazine, and moved to a comfortable reading chair facing the entrance and the research desk. He set his backpack on the floor between his feet, leaning it slightly against his calf, feeling the heft of it as he scanned the paper.

Falling oil prices were being celebrated in the *Atlanta Journal-Constitution*, while in the magazine they were being blamed for the near failure of several smaller European Union economies. A robbery gone wrong in Knoxville had resulted in a hostage situation, and yet another school shooting was reported, this time in a small Michigan town. *Where's the love,* he wondered?

CHAPTER 7

Back at the coffee shop, Tracy was interviewing the barista, Susan, and noting her comments in a small black notebook. She had circled the block and checked in with her two spotters, who had been located in a second floor classroom across the street from the shop. They had seen the man in the khaki's and black shoes leave the coffee shop, and they had seen the accident. And then, unexpectedly, they saw the Cadillac driver finish the job and drive out of their sight. They had taken digital pictures, but there were no license tags on the Cadillac and no identifying marks.

Susan didn't really have any information for Tracy. Yes, she had seen the man walk in. No, it wasn't anyone she'd seen before. No, he didn't speak to her; he just stayed by the door, mostly, looking out at the street. She had stepped into the back, the storage area, to get more coffee filters, and when she came back he had already left.

The line at the coffee shop grew long while Tracy spoke with Susan. One cashier was helping customers, but he was struggling to keep up with the increasing line. Classes were over, and the shop was filling up.

When asked, Susan didn't remember the backpack, or any case or bag for that matter; but she hadn't spent much time thinking about the man. She had been working through her end of the shift checklist, getting a jump on it, and brewing more of the Ethiopian coffee while all this was going on.

"Actually, " Susan said, "you were a lot closer to him than I was. He was blocking your way when you first came in."

Tracy nodded as she finished her notation. She had flipped her badge to the outside of her shirt pocket, where it was more visible and authoritative. "Who else was in here?" she asked.

"Well, the guy with the computer, and that other guy, the one who was sitting there...I saw you talking with him when you came in," said Susan.

"Can you tell me anything about him?" she asked.

"Not really." Susan thought about it for a moment. "He drank the dark, the Ethiopian, and ordered it with room for cream. He was here for about 20 minutes, had an iPad with him, I think. He was reading something."

"How did he pay?" asked Tracy, thinking about credit card numbers.

"Cash, and I gave him a refill," Susan remembered. "Oh, I think he said his name was Zeke. Something like that. Does that help?"

"Zeke...sure, good." she noted this, smiling to herself. "What do you know about the guy with the computer?" asked Tracy.

"He had a small vanilla latte. I think he was watching a movie on his computer. He seemed pretty absorbed in something," added Susan. "Oh, and he paid cash, also. That's all I know...he didn't say much."

"OK," said Tracy. "Please write your name and phone number down for me, Susan. I appreciate your help."

* * *

Zeke looked up and saw the small man, George the assassin, enter the library and immediately move away from the door, to the right and to the cover of the bookshelves, with practiced precision. The man's quick, business-like manner was all that was needed to set off alarms in Zeke's mind. Zeke recognized him from the street in front of the coffee shop, from the accident scene.

In a smooth motion Zeke was out of the chair and behind the nearest shelves with his backpack in tow. *No need to hurry, but keep moving*, he told himself. He set the magazine on a shelf as he worked his way toward the back stairwell. The library stacks were between him and the small man who was still moving laterally while watching the library staff and students, looking for something or someone. Looking for Zeke.

CHAPTER 8

Zeke entered the library stairwell and took the stairs up, two at a time. The small man seemed organized, and Zeke was concerned that the street level exits might be covered. The school library was a three-story building, with stacks and reference on the first two floors, and archives on the top floor.

Entering the archives quietly, and holding the stairwell door to keep it from making a sound as it closed, Zeke moved quietly in his rubber soled Sperry's around the perimeter of the large open room. There were a couple of people at tables, both facing away from the direction he chose.

There were offices around the exterior of the space on three sides, each with glass walls and a wooden door. Zeke found that most were unlocked. The central area was open, housing moveable shelves, tables and chairs and a couple of computer terminals. Zeke moved directly to a vacant corner office, opened the door and closed it quietly behind him. He also shut the wooden blinds. The corner offices had locks on their doors, and he threw the latch.

As is typical in modern office space, the ceiling was a 2'x 2' drop ceiling, with vinyl grid ceiling tiles. The desk chair was on rollers, so Zeke pulled a visitor's chair around the desk to the outside corner of the office. Standing on it, he lifted the corner tile and then the two tiles on either side of it. There was a reinforced ridge that followed the seam of the ceiling where it met the exterior walls. Zeke knew the ridge was the strongest area of the ceiling, closest to the wall attachment hardware.

Quickly, he slid the wrapped bundles above the ceiling tile, spreading them out across several tiles. Then he added the individually wrapped plates. A minute later, he had returned the tiles, repositioned the chair and dusted off the seat. He looked in the center desk drawer for an office key, but had no luck. A small tray in the top right hand drawer held a spare key attached to a paperclip and marked "OD", probably for "Office Door". A moment later, he opened the blinds and went out the office door, careful to check that the key worked, and then locked the latch as he left. It was late Friday afternoon, and most likely the office's occupant wouldn't be back for a while. Staff hours in the library were 9 to 5, Monday through Friday. There was a skeleton staff on weekends but not much going on in the Archive area. He had checked on this during his preparation.

With his empty backpack over his left shoulder, Zeke headed back toward the stairwell.

* * *

A few minutes earlier, George had finished searching the open floors of the library methodically, while looking like someone trying to orient himself in the building. He wandered back to the main door and asked the librarian at the counter an innocuous question. Then he walked through the reading area, looking for Zeke between the stacks as he went.

George decided that the blond man would have to exit the building eventually, so he took a place just outside the main exit door to wait. From there he could see both the main library entrance and the side exit, a self-closing emergency exit door with a push bar that latched on the inside when it closed.

* * *

Tracy Johnson was anxious. Alberto Cruz never showed up. And the guy wearing khakis had been killed in a hit and run and the printer plates had disappeared. And then there was the blond guy. What did Susan say his name was? Tracy checked her notebook. Zeke, that's it, who coincidentally disappeared about the time the bag went missing. And Tracy didn't believe in coincidences.

But, she thought, he was good looking. *Nice eyes. Maybe he'll make my job simple and call me.*

This whole incident began with Alberto Cruz. Alberto Cruz had been an important contact for her unit, a former counterfeiter from the north border of Mexico who had worked for a Mexican cartel that was controlled by a man called Jefe. Jefe's operation was based in San Luis Rio Colorado just south of

Yuma, Arizona.

During their initial interviews, Tracy found out that Cruz was involved in the counterfeiting process in Mexico. He had been recruited into an uneasy partnership with a Mexican cartel, a part of the process of making $100 bills. The cartel members would print the bills and send them over the border. In Phoenix and San Diego and Los Angeles they were delivered to customers in return for real cash, about fifteen cents on the dollar. A bit higher than normal, but the quality of the bogus bills was very good.

Alberto Cruz was not a tall man, but he was substantial. His body type tended toward thick, and with straight, black hair and brown eyes, he had a Mexican-Hispanic look that was supported by his heritage, part European Spanish, part African and a large part Native American. When they first met, Cruz was dressed shabbily, wearing blue pants, a long sleeved, plaid shirt and work boots.

Alberto Cruz had an honest looking face and a sincere manner that somehow instilled confidence in those around him. He seemed concerned about other people, and he was somewhat self-effacing, a quality that enhanced his likability. Cruz wore black-rimmed glasses, nothing fancy, and had small hands with narrow, even elegant fingers. His nails were ragged but clean, and there were no marks or tattoos on them.

There are bad guys, and there are bad guys, but this guy isn't out to hurt anyone, Tracy remembered thinking at the end of the first interview. *He got caught up in this counterfeiting, a victimless crime for the most part. And like a lot of people, it went too quickly, and his family got hurt. Now he wants out. I can understand that.*

When an opportunity finally arose, Cruz told them he had run to Phoenix and then to Atlanta (flown, actually) but was inconveniently spotted by one of Jefe's men, who were checking the outgoing flights from the Phoenix airport. Apparently, he was followed from there, and his place of residence and automobile information were reported back to Jefe in San Luis Rio Colorado. All in return for a few pesos, no doubt.

Cruz was a realist. He had worked closely enough with Jefe's gang to know that he was as good as dead, but he held on to the hope of saving his family. After a couple of days of being followed by some of Jefe's people, he went to the Atlanta police, who in turn called the Secret Service, who passed him on to Tracy's unit.

"I'm Tracy Johnson, Mr. Cruz," Tracy had said at the start of their first interview. "The Atlanta Police have told me an interesting story about you."

"Yes," said Cruz, "I have a curious past. You will want to know what I know," he continued.

"You're being threatened right now?" Tracy continued.

"Yes, I am," said Cruz.

"By whom?" Tracy asked.

"By Jefe. Senor Antonio Gurrerra is his real name. He runs the Mexican gangs in the northern part of my country. He is a violent and unforgiving man," said Cruz.

"What did you bring with you when you left Mexico?" asked Tracy.

"Nothing. I am in danger because I left the work I was doing, and I escaped," said Cruz. "Jefe does not tolerate disobedience."

"Counterfeiting work," Tracy confirmed.

"Yes," said Cruz.

"U.S. dollars," said Tracy.

"Si, yes," said Cruz, nodding.

"What denomination?"

"Sorry?" asked Cruz.

"What size bills? How much? Cuánto?"

"I only know what my part was. I had access to quite a number of the $100 bills."

"How do you know that you're in danger," asked Tracy.

"My nephew, my sister's child, he lived with me in San Luis Rio Colorado. After I left, he was shot dead. He was just a boy, only fifteen years old. And then I received a phone call explaining that the rest of my family was also in danger, unless I gave them what they wanted," said Cruz.

"And you have something that they want?" asked Tracy.

"Well, that may be so," said Cruz with a self-effacing smile.

Tracy had been associated with the Counterfeiting Section for six years, starting shortly after she joined the Secret Service. Two years earlier, after she had been passed over for a promotion that she clearly deserved, she'd had her fill of Washington, DC politics and its snowy weather, and requested a transfer to the Atlanta field office. The transfer had come through with unexpected speed, leaving her with the impression that the desire for her to move on was apparently mutual.

For 137 years the Secret Service had been a part of the

Treasury Department. Their responsibilities, as conceived by President Lincoln were to suppress counterfeit currency after the end of the Civil War. Those responsibilities were expanded in 1901 to include protecting the president, in response to the assassination of President William McKinley. After 9/11, one hundred years later, the Secret Service became a part of the newly formed Department of Homeland Security, along with 21 other federal agencies including TSA, the Coast Guard, FEMA and Customs. The Secret Service has now been in existence for 150 years.

Honestly, Atlanta wasn't a hotbed of counterfeiting activity, and the local Secret Service office spent quite a bit of its time educating local businesses. They focused on banks and retail businesses, and particularly those that handled large amounts of cash. Chasing down criminal enterprises was a very small part of Tracy's day-to-day job. Their offices were more administrative than most law enforcement agencies.

"What else do they want, Mr. Cruz?" asked Tracy. "If they were just getting even with you, I suspect you'd have disappeared already. You said that they know where you're living."

"Where I'm living?" said Cruz.

"Where you're staying in Atlanta."

"Oh, yes, they do," said Cruz.

"What else is there?" asked Tracy again.

"Well, there is the matter of the counterfeit printer plates," said Cruz.

CHAPTER 9

During their interviews, Tracy learned a lot about the counterfeit operation. "Mr. Cruz, how big of an operation are we talking about? What does Jefe gross on the sale of bad currency?"

"Eh, gross?" said Cruz.

"How much does he make?" she asked.

"Once the the plates were finished, he had the ability to print about ten million dollars in counterfeit money," Cruz said.

"Ten million dollars a year?" asked Tracy.

"No, ten million dollars a month," said Cruz. "The thing that limited the production was the paper," he continued. "If he had more paper, he could have printed much more."

"What about the color fibers and the holograms?" asked Tracy.

"Holograms?" asked Cruz. "What is that?"

"Hologramas," said Tracy, referring to her notes.

"Oh, no, Jefe printed bills from 2013, before all of that was changed," said Cruz. "He is very careful, and very smart."

"Where did he get the paper?" she asked.

"I don't know that, Miss Tracy. Trucks delivered it at night. I saw them drive into the warehouse, and the next morning we had a paladar of paper for the printing press."

"Paladar?" asked Tracy.

"You know, rolls of paper on a large wooden frame...for the forklift to move it," said Cruz.

"Pallet?" said Tracy.

"Si, yes, pallet," agreed Cruz.

* * *

Zeke descended the library stairs, passing the second floor and continuing to the street level of the building. He passed no one on the stairs and stepped out the side door into the sunshine. He looked around once, and although he didn't see him, there was a good chance that the small man was nearby. Zeke took out a disposable cell phone and dialed a number from memory. He started across the campus toward the Engineering Building, his phone to his ear.

The call was answered on the second ring. This number was always answered on the second ring. Had it been any different, Zeke would have hung up, wiped his phone electronically, removed the SIM card, and dropped it in the nearest storm sewer.

"4273," said a female voice. She repeated the last four digits that Zeke had dialed but had transposed two numbers, the 7 and the 3. Anyone calling that number would have assumed that they had dialed incorrectly, and a second call to the same number would always go unanswered.

"Hello, Fran," Zeke said. It was Friday, so he used a name that began with an "f". The girl's real name was Sally, and Zeke had known her for two years and six months. Sally was Zeke's primary point of contact while on an assignment with Clive Greene's Agency. She took care of the communications and the coordination of the larger organizational resources for Zeke, and for others, he assumed.

"I have one message," she said with a smile in her voice. "One for you."

"OK," Zeke said. "Go. What's up?"

"They've been looking around, and they're pretty confident that your friend will show up at the party shortly," said Sally. "Just wanted you to know. Anything to pass on?"

Sally was a slender girl, who looked a lot like Marilyn Monroe. She used a wispy Marilyn voice when Zeke called in, which was sometimes amusing. The few times Zeke had seen her, it was obvious that she worked hard to keep her body slim and looking like the actress. Her clothing choices and makeup were, appropriately, retro to the 1950s. Based on what Zeke had seen and heard, though, her IQ had to be near 160.

"Can you let Eric know that I'll be working late tonight, and that I'll try to stop by afterwards?" Eric was their code name for Clive Greene, Zeke's longtime friend and employer.

"Sure, no problem," she said. "Do you think you'll be coming around tomorrow?"

"I'll let you know," he said, "Thanks, Fran." *Thanks, Sally,* he thought.

"OK, bye now," Sally said a second later as the phone went dead.

Zeke pushed the red button on the phone and dropped it in his pocket. He looked around and spotted the small man on the sidewalk behind him, maybe eighty feet back. As he passed a garbage can on the commons, Zeke dropped his empty backpack into it.

Chances are this guy wants the package more than he wants me, Zeke thought.

* * *

After Cruz had been interviewed by the Secret Service team about the counterfeit money, the printer plates and the cartel operation, the Justice Department sent a prosecutor to interview him again, and to discuss a deal with him. He was clearly shaken up.

His appeal to the Atlanta police tended to support his story, and the facts he'd revealed in the interviews about the cartel were consistent with prior knowledge that the Secret Service offices in Washington, DC had confirmed. The DC agents in the counterfeiting section were aware of the influx of U.S. currency from Jefe's operation but had not been able to get anywhere close to the source.

"Mr. Cruz, I'm Julia Roberts," said the Justice Department Prosecutor once they were all seated in the conference room. "No relation."

Cruz looked at her blankly. "Eh?" he said.

There were eight people in the conference room and two sitting just outside, watching body language through the one glass wall and prepared to assist if needed. In the room were Roberts, another attorney from Justice, Fitch, Tracy and Ron, her partner, Cruz and two other local agents, sitting on the eight chairs that surrounded the oblong table. As Roberts explained Cruz's options and legal responsibilities, the agents around the table sat back, some looking at their cell phones, some reading files. Clearly, they felt relieved of the responsibility of Cruz, now that the Justice Department was present. Now, they could relax.

"In exchange for your cooperation, Mr. Cruz," Julia Roberts continued, "we will keep you hidden from Jefe, and we can convince the INS to allow you to stay in the country. After we arrest Jefe and his team, after the trial, we can arrange for you to join witness protection. You can start a new life from there."

"Si," said Cruz.

"And for now, you'll want to abandon the house you've rented, and we'll put you up in a hotel room for the rest of this week." Roberts paused and looked at some papers for a minute. "Can we get the cameras rolling, now?" she asked Fitch. He nodded and signed to one of the agents sitting at the table.

CHAPTER 10

Zeke Traynor had disappeared into the Engineering Building after spotting the small man and disposing of the backpack on the campus green. Watching carefully, he walked near and seemingly with a small group of male students intent on getting someplace important. *Maybe a study group, or a classroom for an evening class,* he thought.

As he mirrored their pace and direction, Zeke was able to hear their conversation taking place about six feet away. "I think the cosmological constant has to be included, since space creates energy as it expands," said someone with very thick glasses and a cowlick in his short, greasy brown hair. "It just makes sense, if we're ever going to be able to measure the acceleration of the universe's expansion."

"Yeah," replied another awkward looking boy, "but you've got to accept that space is not 'nothing' for that to be true."

Physics, thought Zeke, *sounds like astrophysics. Einstein's Gravity Theory. A discarded theory, one that Einstein himself refuted later on. But it's being revisited,* thought Zeke. *Let's see,* he thought, *Einstein said, 'Gravity is not a force. It's a curve in space-time.' Ah, there's still hope. He may not have to give back his Nobel Prize after all.* Zeke smiled to himself.

The central hallway in the engineering building was wide, with a very high ceiling, which created a lot of volume and a sense of separation, even though he stayed close to the group of students. The discussion turned more mundane, about homework assignments and study times as Zeke veered off from the group and entered what appeared to be an area of administrative offices. Through the glass wall he had seen two women behind their desks still working, and he noticed that posted hours ended at 7PM weekdays. Most likely, that was to give professors an opportunity to take care of administrative items after classes were over.

"Hello, ladies," Zeke said as he entered their office and moved away from the front wall and door. "Can you help me? I'd like to leave a message for Dr. Gordon." He'd noticed the name tattooed on a door he had passed on his walk through the building, as well as on the small plastic card showing the face of a clock set for 9:30, hanging from the door. *9:30 AM,* he thought.

"Sure can," said the larger of the two women, without looking up. "There's note paper on the counter, there, and a pen. Write what you want, and we'll make sure he gets it."

Zeke grabbed a piece of message paper and a pen, and then turned so he could see the bodies passing through the engineering building's first floor corridor. He slid into a small, empty desk to write the note, a move that made him much less visible to the passersby. A few minutes later, he handed the folded note to the nearest woman. It said, "Dr. Gordon" on the outside. Inside he had scribbled an innocuous question, deliberately vague with the note unsigned. Zeke left the office area. There had been enough time during that intermission to determine that he wasn't being followed. At least not by anyone he recognized. Foot traffic continued to flow, and Zeke didn't see anyone loitering in the hall.

There are some advantages to an eidetic memory. Zeke had always been able to remember faces, things, events and facts with little difficulty. And although his original aptitude appeared to have been more left brained and analytical, he had worked hard to create a balance by studying and researching some very right-brained things. Art, history, music and languages were among them. One reason that Zeke was originally recruited for the Army's Military Intelligence Civilian Excepted Career Program was his mastery of Spanish and Arabic as a second and third language.

Zeke had chosen his language studies pragmatically. Spanish is the primary language in 21 countries, and Arabic is the primary language in 26 countries. Combined with English, these languages gave him fluency in the primary language of 101 countries, 101 of the 195 countries of the world. Well, 196 countries of the world, if you counted Taiwan.

Along with that, these languages were common denominators spoken in a number of the remaining countries of the world. All of which made being fluent in the three of them a measurable advantage in his former line of work, his work with MICECP.

The Military Intelligence Civilian Excepted Career Program, called "MIC" by those involved in the program, is run out of Fort Meade in Maryland, exactly twenty-three miles from the White House front door. The name of the program is confusing, but the intent is clear. The civilians employed in this program are actively recruited, trained, and assigned to conduct highly specialized operational intelligence functions within the Army. They work worldwide and with a huge emphasis on counterintelligence. And, because of their civilian status, they can do what Army personnel can't. Zeke had been recruited at the inception of the program in 2008, and he spent 5 years as an operative for MIC before he retired to private life.

With no one following him, and being in no visible danger, Zeke turned right from the office and continued through the building and then out onto the campus. He circled around off campus and took a circumfluous route that led back to the Enclave. As he approached the apartment complex, he circled it twice from a distance of about 75 yards, saw no one that looked like his library shadow, and then carefully let himself in through a locked side door.

No one in the stairwell, no one in the hallway, four steps to the door and he pulled up fast, his hand almost grabbing the exterior door handle before pulling back. The "tell" that Zeke left on his outside door was missing, indicating that someone had opened the door at least one time.

They're either in there waiting, or in there searching, or they've already come and gone, he thought. *I've been gone thirty-eight minutes, which lends probability to the likelihood that they're still inside.*

He braced himself and turned the door handle slowly. It was unlocked.

CHAPTER 11

Zeke quickly looked around the apartment's exterior hallway. He was alone. He released the door handle and moved quickly and quietly to the maintenance closet, the one he had unlocked that morning. In addition to electrical boxes, fire sprinkler pipes and cable risers, Zeke found the toolbox sitting in the corner. He hefted a two-pound hammer and slipped a medium sized Phillips head screwdriver into his pants pocket.

At the apartment door again, Zeke used his left hand to turn the handle, while holding the unlocked door closed. The hammer was in his right hand, to be used either as a projectile, a distraction or a close-combat weapon. Zeke threw the door open suddenly, and slid into the apartment, low and quick but without losing his footing. He looked left and right as he passed the kitchen and then the open bedroom door. He saw no one.

He scanned the furniture and the far walls of the open floor plan living area. The blinds were drawn; and the two rented canvas paintings still adorned the walls. The bookshelf and recliner were on the right side of the room, near the window.

The leather couch was to the left, with a glass coffee table in front of it. Sitting on the left end of the leather couch, watching quietly, was Alberto Cruz. Zeke relaxed.

Alberto smiled at him. "Mister Zeke," he said, sounding a little bit like 'Meester'. "Good to see you again. Bienvenido a casa."

Zeke walked to the other end of the leather sofa and set the hammer on the coffee table, carefully to avoid scratching it. He pulled the screwdriver from his pocket and set it next to the first tool, both out of Cruz's reach. Then he walked to the straight-backed chair opposite the sofa and propped himself on the front edge of it, leaning in a bit, looking at Cruz.

"Mister Cruz, hello," said Zeke. "That was unexpected. You disappearing like that was odd, particularly since you'd hired us to protect you. What happened?"

"I think you call it intuition," said Cruz. "I was preparing for the exchange earlier this afternoon and I suddenly felt as if someone had…how do you say…stepped on my grave. Have you had that feeling? It unnerved me. I had to get away from the situation."

"Who was the accident victim?" Zeke asked.

"I saw that on the television. An unfortunate man," said Cruz. "That was Roberto Estido. He is my neighbor down the street, about my size. Earlier today I offered him $100 to dress in the beige pants and black shoes, and to take the backpack to the coffee shop and give it to the man who was to meet me there. I had no idea that he would be run over!"

"He left the money and the printer plates," said Zeke, "The

Secret Service can't be happy with the way things turned out. Who spooked you, Alberto?" he asked.

"The small man, George, the Accountant, I thought I saw him. I went to the campus early, maybe two o'clock, and went to the coffee shop. I walked the area and sat and drank an espresso. And then, as I was leaving the campus, I saw him, I felt him. I've seen him before with Jefe, and I want nothing to do with him." Cruz added, "El es el diablo."

* * *

"Money would be no use to a dead man," Cruz said. He squirmed and fidgeted in his seat, looking up and to the right, and pausing in thought as he responded to Zeke Traynor's questions.

Zeke had said, "Why did you disappear?"

"I was reminded of a greater risk," he said.

Zeke didn't like Alberto Cruz. He remained formally polite and they conversed, but he felt no trust or connection with the man. Cruz was clearly thinking only of his own interests, and as such, he was unpredictable and unreliable. The information Cruz traded in seemed a bit off balance, a bit incomplete.

But Cruz had spent a week with the Secret Service agents, a week inside their building in interviews and planning sessions and generally just staying close to them. It was a form of self-imposed protective custody that Cruz had designed to keep Jefe's people away from him. And while he was with the Secret Service agents, he'd watched and learned.

He'd observed their interactions, their hierarchy, their

pecking order. He watched their chain of command, and listened to their phone calls. He watched and memorized, as the agents, keeping him close for protection, became more relaxed and informal within their own environment, within their open offices. The office was set up as a bullpen, with cubical type arrangements and low walls, and cabinets and shelving around the outside walls. One wall housed the offices of senior team members, with glass windows from the waist up, and faux wood blinds and closing doors.

During that week, he had heard their phone calls, witnessed their schedules and heard their personal cell phone calls to and from their family and friends. They didn't necessarily trust him, and they didn't necessarily not trust him. They viewed their responsibility as one of protection and of coordination of the efforts to find and arrest the threat to Cruz, Jefe's man.

Cruz had played dumb, and he'd done it well. He had acted fairly simple and ignorant- peasant-like- and had spoken in somewhat broken English while around the agents. Often in their hours of interviewing, Cruz feigned ignorance of the English language, and ignorance of the answers to the questions they asked him. He found it easier to corrupt the interviews using a slight language barrier as a buffer and a tool. It gave him a couple of seconds extra to think. He used pauses and clarifications, questions, definitions and supposed misunderstanding to obfuscate the interviews and create an unbalanced flow. The agents seemed excited to have Cruz in hand, and they seemed ready to believe his story.

The information about Tracy was given to Zeke when Cruz

first hired The Agency for his own protection. In planning for the exchange with the Secret Service, Cruz also quietly arranged for Clive's operation to provide private protection, in case the federal agents weren't enough. Cruz had mentioned to Zeke that Tracy was Secret Service, that she was allergic to dog and cat hair (Cruz had overheard her talking to a friend), and that she carried a 9mm Glock 26 in her purse (he'd seen the gun).

In the end, Cruz knew as much about the Atlanta Secret Service agents and their families and their habits as they knew about him. Possibly he knew more.

"Our next step will need to be to re-establish contact and then set up another exchange," said Zeke.

Alberto Cruz leaned forward and set his coffee cup on the table in front of him. Then he leaned back again and turned a bit toward Zeke. Cruz was a clever man.

"You were hoping that the Secret Service would arrest the small man," said Zeke. "That you could avoid the situation altogether, right?"

Alberto smiled.

"So," said Zeke with a smile, "Alberto, are you an honest man?"

Deception research was a study that MICECP had engineered. Although body language and facial expressions have long been thought of as a key to identifying honesty, they don't provide reliable or necessarily consistent results across a number of different people. Knowing a person well can increase the odds of its effectiveness, but different people react differently as they participate in deceit.

Recent research indicated that there's a better way to identify lies. With unconventional questions and acute listening. Zeke was well trained in this technique.

"Si, yes," said Cruz helpfully. "I am honest."

"Tell me about your journey to Atlanta," said Zeke. "But tell it in reverse."

Cruz looked confused. "Reverse? You mean backwards?" he asked.

"Sure, start with your arrival here today, and tell me what happened, in reverse."

"But why?" asked Cruz.

"Humor me," said Zeke.

"What?"

"OK, so you're here now, and you hired us to protect you. What happened before you contacted The Agency?" asked Zeke. "What prompted you to contact us?"

"I had rented a house, and I was very careful. No one was supposed to know where I was, not even my cousins. But in spite of that, I was contacted by the small man, the Accountant," said Cruz.

"You were supposed to go to a meeting at the coffeeshop?" Zeke prompted.

"Yes, the Secret Service agents moved me to a hotel room so I would be safe, and they set up to watch me at the meeting, the exchange. They gave me back the printing plates to return to the small man, and they were planning to arrest him."

"But..." said Zeke.

"But, I was very frightened. I wasn't convinced that the agents could protect me."

"You'd spent the week with the Secret Service, right?" asked Zeke.

"Yes, right after the time I was contacted by Jefe's men, I went to the police and explained my situation. I told them that I had escaped from Mexico and had been involved in counterfeiting. They said that there was maybe a crime, but it was in a different country, and they took me to meet with the Secret Service agents. They seemed to think that I wanted to leave, but in truth, I wanted to stay with them, surrounded by their agents, for as long as possible."

"Why?" asked Zeke.

"Because, one does not cross Jefe and expect there to be no consequences. I escaped with my life and their money and the printer plates, which means that I'm in serious trouble."

"And you called us," said Zeke.

"Yes, after I heard from George, the Accountant, last week I contacted your Agency. I felt that I needed protection from Jefe's men," said Cruz. "I don't have confidence that the Secret Service agents are enough. In Mexico, it is not unusual to hire private protection. The police are barely adequate, and many are very corrupt."

"So, working backwards, before you heard from Jefe's man, the Accountant..." Zeke asked.

"I had a visit from two other men about a week or so ago. They were not violent men, but they made it known that they were from Jefe, and were here in Atlanta to resolve the situation."

"To retrieve the plates?" asked Zeke.

"Well, yes, and the money, of course. And me, honestly."

"You?" asked Zeke.

"Well, yes."

"Why would they want to take you back, Alberto?" asked Zeke.

"Oh. Well, actually, I am the artist," said Cruz.

"The counterfeiting artist?" asked Zeke. "The forger?"

"Si," said Cruz. "I just haven't told anyone about that part."

CHAPTER 12

The small man, George, examined the backpack again. He carefully opened each outside pocket, expanded it to its full size with the fingers of his left hand, and shined the flashlight into the opening. Looking for uneven stitching, a torn seam, possibly a small opening. Then he unzipped the zipper around the circumference of the pack and repeated the search inside the compartments.

He'd found a small pad and a couple of pens in one pocket, and he'd noticed some chewing gum in another pocket. But there was no sign of the plates or the money. He used both hands to pull at the seams inside the pack, straining them away from each other, in search of a hidden compartment or pocket.

The stitching was made up of big, wide stitches of nylon, apparently run over twice with a sewing machine to assure a solid seam. The backpack had an almost nautical feel to it, with the nylon and canvas exterior, the large stitching and the nylon rope drawstrings. There was a label inside, a brand that George had never seen before. It contained a simple logo, which seemed to illustrate water with a sailboat floating on top of it, and which said only, "Aft Creations".

George could tell immediately by the feel of the bag- its heft- that neither the plates nor the money were hidden in it. But more than once he had found an important piece to the puzzle he was working on by paying attention to a seemingly innocuous item. And it gave him a sense of his new prey, the man he'd taken it from.

For example, George knew from what he'd seen in the backpack that the blond man was organized and efficient, that he wanted to be anonymous, and that he was rather minimalist. Combined with his observations of the blond man earlier, George was developing a mental picture of a competent man, in good shape and able to respond or react quickly to unexpected stimuli. He was a man to be cautious around.

Having searched the entire bag, every pocket and compartment twice, George took the X-acto knife from the desk and began gently cutting the seams away from the bag. A few minutes later, there were individual pieces of the bag lying in an organized fashion across the desk. Each piece was reexamined, and then set aside in a pile of discards. There was nothing else here, he decided.

George was nothing if not meticulous. He spent much of his time thinking and reliving situations from various perspectives and with a variety of emphases, culling out details and possibilities, and constructing scenarios to accommodate most any unexpected situation.

"If it's not in here," he thought aloud, "then where might it be?"

George was sitting at the desk in his hotel room next to the Olympic Park. From his upper floor room he had a view of the Interstate. Lost in thought, he watched the traffic slowly crawling by. It was rush hour, and evening was near.

* * *

Tracy Johnson was watching the traffic, too. Thinking black thoughts, she snapped her pencil in frustration. Sitting at her Steelcase desk in her Homeland Security office on Spring Street, less than a mile and a half south of the Georgia Tech campus, she was anxious to find Cruz and the plates, and to wrap this case up. She'd thought that they were close, and then it went sideways in a major way with the hit and run.

Tracy reached out unconsciously and touched the butt of her Glock, which she was wearing in a reversed holster on her left hip. She then touched the pocket that held her badge and ID; at some subliminal level, she found this reassuring.

Fitch was stepping into the case, taking some control away from her, and thinking in terms of possible damage control. He had started showing up at team meetings and insisted on being kept current on the situation, several times a day.

So, Tracy thought, *where's the invisible planet?* She subscribed to the astronomers' theory that the gravitational forces of planets that couldn't be seen acted on the orbit and behavior of visible planets. So one could essentially triangulate the existence of the invisible body by observing its effect on its neighboring planets and their moons. Applied to law enforcement, this theory could translate to determining the cause of an action- such as Cruz never coming to the coffee shop- by looking at what might be happening to motivate him in that direction. *What are the important gravitational influences on Mr. Cruz*, she thought. This type of postulation often led to a series of "What if...?" questions.

Like, What if Cruz saw something that motivated him to run? To run and to take the money and the plates, that is. Maybe the plates were never in that backpack, and that's why it had to disappear. What would have caused that reaction?

Tracy doodled with the sharp end of the broken pencil and a legal pad that was sitting on her desk. She wrote, "Fear". *That would be the most effective motivator,* she thought. *Fear of what, though, or of whom?*

Or, what if Cruz never intended to return the plates to Jefe or his men? Had he been using the Secret Service all this time, setting them up for his escape with the plates? Cruz had insisted that, for credibility, the plates must be in the backpack when he met with Jefe's men. And he'd insisted that they be the originals. When Cruz refused to make the exchange without them, Tracy's boss Fitch had finally complied.

Tracy knew that Cruz had run from the Mexican cartel, and had taken the money and the printer plates with him. She knew, from Cruz, that they had killed a member of his family in retribution. His nephew in San Luis Rio Colorado, Pablo, a fifteen-year-old boy. They killed him because he was related to Cruz. When Cruz arrived at Secret Service headquarters, he was obviously upset.

When Cruz had been found in the Phoenix airport, his presence was reported back to Jefe. They had dogged him in Atlanta after that, letting him know that they had found him, toying with him, making him wait. But they stayed with him, kept him in sight until he was good and scared. They used the safety of his family in Mexico as a threat, and then they demanded the counterfeiting plates in return for his family's safety.

When he'd first told the story to Tracy and her partner, he was resigned. Cruz said that he knew that it was just a matter of time. But he had information about the Mexicans, about their operations and the counterfeiting.

"How long did you work for the cartel?" Tracy had asked.

"Most of my life, I guess," said Alberto Cruz. "Since I was a young man, my Uncle saw my talent and he mentioned it to Jefe. I went from the fishing boat to the warehouse in San Luis Rio Colorado. That warehouse was my home for many years."

* * *

So, Cruz was already scared about the drop, and if fear was the motivator, then how did it become so amped up that it made him skip the meeting? She wrote, "Skipped" on the pad. Then she wrote, "Counterfeit printer plates".

The counterfeit plates and the money were specific requests by Jefe's men. Someone had contacted Cruz on his cellphone, someone who spoke in Cruz's native dialect and with some of his hometown colloquialisms. The voice had spelled it out to him last Saturday afternoon. Get the money and the printer plates together, and have them ready to deliver. "Dispone de una semana," "you have one week," the voice had said, and hung up.

Tracy wrote "Greed" on the paper next, a new column heading. If Cruz had found a partner, the plates could have been snatched after the man in khaki's had left the coffee shop. Maybe the blond guy, Zeke, or someone outside, just stepping in for a moment and back out with the backpack. It would take about three seconds.

If Cruz masterminded this whole scene, he may have disappeared himself again, but this time with the counterfeit plates. Perhaps he intended to bargain them away in return for his life.

There were no further reports, though, from Secret Service Headquarters in DC. Nor had she heard anything from the Yuma Border Patrol Sector. The intelligence that they had gathered so far tended to support Cruz's testimony about the Mexican cartel and its leadership. In fact, from what was shared with Tracy and Ron, this Jefe was a very bad man.

Cruz was in a bind when he first approached the Atlanta police. He was being watched, and the Mexicans following him knew about his car and his house. *It's possible,* she thought, *that he used the time in the Homeland Security Building to insulate himself and plan a final escape.*

Tracy's phone rang. She checked the caller ID and saw that it was Ron. She answered, "Yea, Ron, what's up?"

Tracy's partner, Ron Marcus, had spent the week organizing and coordinating this effort. The logistics of the drop were his responsibility, while Tracy was sticking with Cruz, interviewing him, preparing him. She had been working in tandem with two other agents, focused on Cruz for the best part of the week.

Marcus was a tall, fit man who moved a lot like a dancer, mostly on the balls of his feet. It looked odd until you got used to it. His thin frame accentuated his large head, nose and ears. She'd found him to be deceptively quick and prone to action. He eschewed the desk part of the job, looking for reasons to get back out to the field whenever he could.

A soft-spoken voice said, "Trace, I'm following up on a lead, trying to figure out how the plates and the money disappeared. We've been canvasing the buildings around the coffee shop. I kind of feel like Cruz had this whole thing set up, ready to pull a Houdini on us. Seems like he's in the wind. But I found a kid who was sitting at a table, outside the coffee shop when this went down. I don't think you saw him out there. He was sort of off to one side, and he had his books out on one of their umbrella tables. Studying for a test. I think he may have seen more than he knows."

About time we caught a break, thought Tracy. But she knew that the likelihood of any one lead panning out was sparse.

"Do you want me to meet you to interview him now?" she asked. The presence of two agents in an interview sometimes had the effect of illustrating the serious nature of the questions, and creating a somber tone. Two authoritative figures represent a commitment to the proceedings.

"No, I've made the initial contact," Ron said. "But we should interview him again tomorrow morning, in the office. I told him to stop by at 8:00 AM to chat with us again."

"OK, good. You think the kid saw something?" Tracy asked hopefully.

"He claims that most of the time he was in his books, but he had a good vantage point to see everything that happened. Said that he saw a guy who looked Hispanic leave the coffee shop and walk down the street in front of him. Said he looked up, but the guy didn't make eye contact. Then the guy crossed the street and got in the middle of the accident. This kid, Mike Williams is his name, by the way, he also said that after the guy passed by and was hit by the car, he noticed an older lady, walking back and forth on the street in front of the shop, walking quickly and talking on her phone."

That would be me, thought Tracy. "Clothing?"

"He said black leggings and a yellow shirt, so, yeah, it sounds like you, 'older lady.'" Ron made a noise that sounded like a chuckle.

CHAPTER 13

"How're you doing, my friend?" asked Clive.

"It was a bit of a surprise, the hit and run," Zeke commented. "Unexpected, and right on top of Cruz sending in a substitute." They were sitting at a tall table in a restaurant near the Tech campus.

Clive sipped his beer. It was a black and tan. The server brought Zeke a glass of a local IPA and set it in front of him. Zeke tasted the draught and nodded to the server.

"Indeed," said Clive. "It sounds like that hit and run was a bit of nasty business."

"Nasty enough, right?" Zeke sipped. "Time for a change of fortune."

"Change of fortune" was a term that Zeke and Clive used at their former jobs, where they had met seven years ago. They met while working at 'MIC'. Zeke had been highly recruited for counterintelligence in the group, and Clive, an MI-6 Operative, was on loan to the program.

Zeke's job had been as an operative at the Military Intelligence

Civilian Excepted Career Program in Fort Meade, Maryland. The name of the program has always seemed vague, and perhaps that was intentional. The MICECP is charged with developing a highly qualified, technically skilled, foreign language capable workforce for intelligence and counterintelligence missions worldwide.

The Army wanted intelligence and counterintelligence operatives that they could move around to various hotspots worldwide, and who could provide intelligence to various Army commands. The reason they opted for civilian operatives was, in Zeke's opinion, that there weren't enough soldiers that have the skill set necessary to complete that mission statement. And the Army is a government bureaucracy, which means that ranks, pay grades, personnel records, logistical support, supplies and all of that would be controlled by other branches of the Army.

Zeke's belief was that, by using a civilian program, the Intelligence and Security Command guys would have much more direct control. The program was started in 2008, the year he was recruited.

Another benefit of using civilian talent like Zeke was that there are fewer restrictions. The FBI, for example, is authorized to work only within the United States, and the CIA is authorized to work only outside of the United States. Operatives in the MICECP program can do either, and in the war on terrorism, the geographic boundaries are indistinct.

The website for the program says, "Army commands worldwide can avail themselves of this unique talent pool to meet their mission-essential requirements." In the beginning, the operatives were mostly current-day mercenaries with combat experience, language skills and intelligence training. A number of the guys that he had worked with were recently discharged soldiers who had seen action in Afghanistan, Iraq or Pakistan. They went through training and were deployed around the globe to various hotspots.

Paired together, Clive and Zeke worked counterintelligence, personal protection details, and counterterrorism. They handled the ransom exchange in a high profile international kidnapping, handled bomb threats against U.S. companies abroad and performed a myriad of other similar activities.

When the program began in 2008, Zeke had been hired as one of the first Intelligence Operations Specialists, a civilian contractor to the Army. He worked there until 2014. Zeke was prone to action. His experience and training was aimed at anticipating situations and taking evasive or preemptive action without hesitation. But he also knew how to modify his personality to reflect the person he was interviewing, developing an empathetic and relatable persona that was usually attractive to the others involved. He knew how to become likable.

"Change of fortune" meant that the momentum was due to shift in their favor, and in practice it often did. It wasn't a tangible event, but when it was happening, there was a sense of change in the air, even an excitement. Like a momentum shift in an American football game.

"We arranged for your backup, a watcher," said Clive. It wasn't unusual for The Agency to hire undercover operatives to stand by in case an operation went sideways. Typically, a watcher remained on the sidelines, but monitored the situation, communicating with The Agency directly, and remaining available in case plans changed. It was a practice that had paid off more than once in the past.

"Had a bit of a revelation, today," said Zeke.

"What's that?" asked Clive.

"It turns out that Cruz is actually the artist. The forger," said Zeke.

"That's unexpected, I suppose," said Clive.

"Indeed," said Zeke. "I'm not sure he meant to admit it. But, I was interviewing him, and it came out. He said that he just hadn't told anyone yet."

"He seems to be a man with many talents, and an extraordinary penchant for luck," said Clive.

"I agree," said Zeke. Both men thought in silence for a second.

"My neighbor said something odd today," Zeke continued.

"Like what?"

"Well, I've told you about Kimmy. She's a bit different, like some of the people in that cult we encountered down in Brazil," he continued. "She definitely has her own understanding of the way everything works."

"OK." Clive's beer was gone. He waved and smiled at the server, indicating his empty glass.

"She was talking about the hit and run I saw, and she said, 'When something like that happens, evil is always nearby and involved.' And based on our experience, there's a lot of truth to that, Clive."

"The older I get, the less I'm inclined to dismiss that kind of talk," Clive said.

"There was a guy there outside the coffee shop, a small guy, and I passed him as I was trying to catch up to the man who was hit by the car. It was peripheral, but I remember noticing that his eyes were almost reptilian. They didn't blink, and when I stepped past him, I felt a cold chill. At the time I was in a hurry to get to the bag's owner. And then the car jumped in front of me and killed him."

"Contract hit?" asked Clive.

"Almost certainly. At first it seemed pretty random, but then there was the double-tap and the car driving off after the accident. So, yes, most likely a contract."

"Talk to the police?" Clive asked.

"Not yet. The locals were too busy at the scene, and they told everyone to clear the street. Secret Service was there, too." Zeke sipped his beer and pushed it aside, half empty.

"Thanks for the beer, Clive," said Zeke. "We'll want to stand by to reschedule the exchange with Mr. Cruz as soon as possible."

They shook hands and Zeke walked out. The waitress approached and looked at Clive questioningly. She was a pretty blonde woman, approaching middle age, and a regular at this restaurant. She didn't wear a wedding ring.

"How late are you working tonight, Darlene?" asked Clive.

"I'm off in half an hour," she said with a smile.

"Shepard's Pie, then?" he asked.

"Certainly," said the waitress.

"And, after that, would you want a ride?" asked Clive.

"Perhaps so," she said with a smile.

Clive stayed to finish his dinner and his beer.

CHAPTER 14

On Saturday morning, Tracy had decided to observe her partner's interview of the Williams kid from the other side of the one-way glass. If she felt it would be a benefit, she could always enter the room and join the questioning later. But it may be that the kid would be forthcoming and cooperative, in which case there would be no need to pressure him.

She had arrived at the witness room the following morning at about 8:15, after Ron had started his questioning. The boy, obviously a student, and probably a freshman or sophomore, based upon his young looks and awkward posture, was sitting on one side of the table with a glass of something in front of him. Almost clear, like Mountain Dew, she noticed, with a slight yellow tint. Ron had a paper cup of coffee, top on and with a cardboard burn protector circling the upper third of the cup. He was holding the cup, sipping at it while they talked.

"So, tell me again, Mike Williams," Ron said, "What did you see?"

"That was the worst thing I've ever seen," said Mike. "Man, I was studying calculus, so I didn't really see much. I saw a guy go into the coffee shop with a backpack. I did notice him, because it happened as I was getting my stuff organized, and he bumped my table as he walked by. Said he was sorry when I looked up, but he kept going, didn't make eye contact."

"What did he look like?" Ron asked.

"Well, like I said, he looked Hispanic, I guess. Sort of short and stocky, and with thick black hair. He didn't have an accent, though. I remember thinking that I expected an accent and there wasn't any."

"Can you remember the color of his eyes?" Ron asked.

"Seems like they were dark," Mike said.

"Any tattoos or marks you noticed on this guy?" asked Ron. "Maybe on his face or neck?"

"No, I don't remember any," Mike said. "He was wearing khakis and a blue shirt. I only saw him for a second, and then again when he left."

"Which way did he go when he left the shop?" asked Ron.

"He turned the opposite way and walked out into the street, away from me. Then the car flew by me and crushed him. Man, that was bad. I wasn't focused on it, but later when you asked, it seemed a little bit odd to me that he came in from one direction, and left in another. Unless he was on his way somewhere, and just stopped in for a cup of coffee to take with him. Lotsa guys do that, I think."

Ron nodded, and asked about the backpack. Tracy could see the kid's head start shaking, back and forth. No.

The interview went on for another half hour before Tracy

left, but there wasn't much else that came to light. Ron had walked him through the chronology and then revisited the key points, but without uncovering anything further.

The investigation is slowing way down, thought Tracy. It had been about 16 hours since the victim walked out of the coffee shop, and they had nothing to show, no information, no leads, no clues. *Alright, lets start over,* she thought. *Let's start at the beginning.*

So, Cruz contacts the Atlanta police, who in turn contact the Secret Service and Ron and Tracy are assigned to handle him. Cruz showed up about a week ago, looking for help and a way out. He was visibly shaken when he was escorted into their offices. Ron signed for him, which released the Atlanta uniform cops from responsibility, and they left.

"Wait, what are you doing?" Cruz had said to the Atlanta uniform. "I need you to protect me. They're coming after me, and they'll kill me."

"Can't really do anything about that until a crime is committed," said the younger policeman. "People get threatened all the time, but usually its just noise. You can hire a bodyguard if you're really worried."

"Well, what are you here for, then?" asked Cruz.

"We're here to protect and serve," said the older cop as they turned and left.

Then there was a long morning of meetings with Cruz with various other agents coming and going, and then half a day verifying the facts. Finally, with Cruz still in protective custody of a fashion and sitting in their offices between meetings – they began to arrange for the exchange to be made, while Cruz secretly arranged with The Agency for protection.

It wasn't easy, and it certainly wasn't routine, gathering together the printer plates and the money, keeping both low-key and secure.

During that workweek, Cruz observed a number of agents. He was sitting at a vacant desk that Wednesday past when a cell phone rang in the office nearby. "Martino," answered the agent that Cruz knew to be Tom Martino, a tall, thin man who looked to be about 40 years old. Martino paused and then said, "How are you, honey?"

Cruz couldn't hear the other end of the conversation, but by this time he knew that Martino was chatting with his daughter, a middle school student. She called every day when she got home from school, which Cruz assumed was because she was alone in the house. Either Martino's wife worked, or he was a single dad.

"I don't know if I can get off tomorrow morning," Martino continued. He had dark brown hair, cut short and wore a white shirt, with his cuffs rolled up two turns. His sports coat was on the back of his chair. "I have to work."

Martino listened for a moment. "Of course, I'd love to see you get the award, hon. I'm just not sure that I can get out to the school in time. But I'll check and see about it. We can talk about it when I get home, OK?"

Cruz made a mental note of the man's situation and filed it away with his many recent observations of the Secret Service agents' behaviors.

* * *

The next day the man who had first called him, the small man, George, contacted Cruz and set up the exchange at the coffee shop. Friday afternoon, around 4:50 PM, the man was to meet him at the shop, collect the blue and gray backpack, and part ways. That Cruz had substituted a surrogate was out of character from what Tracy knew. Perhaps he'd found a Judas goat, one to take his place—a distraction while he planned an escape.

And it seems to have worked. He's vanished, she thought.

CHAPTER 15

At that same moment, in the border town of San Luis Rio Colorado, Sonora, Mexico, in a large house, in a large and protected compound, Antonio Herman Gurrerra heard his cell phone ring. He was a tall, slim man, taller than most of his relatives, perhaps the result of an errant gene a couple of generations back. Possibly this was the result of a liaison between his grandmother and a tall, handsome soldier during the Second World War.

Antonio was, however, a man of action. He had learned that action quells fear, action brings results, and that quick and decisive action can be crippling to his opponents—the quicker, the better.

The display on his cell phone said that the caller was "indisponible", or unavailable, which wasn't true at all, was it? The caller was very available; all Antonio needed to do was answer the phone. The calling number was, however, "unavailable", and he decided that was probably the message the phone company was trying to send.

He answered.

"Rápidamente," he said, quietly.

"Jefe, hello," said the voice.

He listened for twenty-five seconds and hung up. Three young children were playing loudly in the next room. It sounded like they were playing La Gallinita Ciega, the Blind Hen, running and yelling to each other in excitement. With three, there was always the odd man out, and always the partnership by the end of the games. Antonio had usually been the odd man out in his youth. But not so much anymore.

He turned around and saw Carlos standing in the open archway between the rooms. From there, Carlos could survey and protect both rooms, as well as the immediate outdoor area, visible through windows and large sliding glass doors in the family room where the bambinos were playing. Carlos had slung his AR-15 over his shoulder, and it was presently arranged across his back. *Easy access to such an ugly weapon*, thought Antonio.

The AR-15 is a semi-automatic rifle that shoots a .223 Remington or a 5.56 NATO cartridge. Antonio knew that Carlos favored the NATO bullets, which were 45 mm and travelled at about 14 meters per second. This one wasn't a short barrel model, and there was lots of stopping power there.

The call came from his brother, Enrique, who had been overseeing a shipment of heroine. The box had been wrapped in coffee grounds, to prevent the dogs from identifying its contents, and shipped FedEx to a vacant Los Angeles address. The address was directly across the street from a home owned by Gurrerra, but held in a relative's name. Once delivered to the vacant house, the neighbor across the street would arrange to pick it up, unwrap it in a different location, and distribute the product through their usual channels. There were hundreds of similar deliveries that took place each month across the country.

Enrique called to confirm the package had arrived, and that there had been no activity in the area in the days before the delivery. It had been taken to the warehouse and was being divided up for distribution. A few of his more distant relatives – cousins mostly – were involved at this point. It was business as usual.

The matter with Cruz should be coming to an end soon, Antonio thought. He preferred to use family members for such activities because their loyalty was assured, with their families and their possessions remaining back in Mexico. But this George fellow was quite good and had been very efficient in the past. El Contador, the Accountant, he was called. This was a sticky situation, and a professional was certainly called for. Not inexpensive, but considering the potential loss of face and respect, it was important to control the situation with quick and decisive action.

* * *

Zeke Traynor had just finished a late Saturday breakfast and was sitting at his kitchen island among the remnants and the dishes. Breakfast had been two eggs and bacon, a good dose of protein, along with a few carbs in the form of rye toast, and coffee. It put Zeke in mind of the breakfasts that his mother used to make for him on Saturday mornings.

He decided to call Tracy Johnson.

"Hi, this is Tracy," she said, responding to the unfamiliar number on her buzzing personal smartphone.

"Tracy, hi, this is Zeke Traynor. We met in the coffee shop on campus last night. You were looking for your dog." She could hear the smile in Zeke's voice.

"Oh, right," she said. "Uh, have you found him?"

"I thought you said it was a 'her,'" teased Zeke, still smiling. "But no matter, I haven't found the dog."

"Oh," said Tracy.

"Well, listen," Zeke continued, "I think we have a mutual acquaintance. After you stopped by my table I got to thinking about it."

"Yes?" asked Tracy, remembering his interesting eyes, but thinking that this was a bad time for a new relationship. A whole lot had happened to distract her since she'd given Zeke her phone number yesterday afternoon.

"Don't be upset about this, OK? I'm in town working on a project with Clive Greene. I think you may know Clive, or perhaps your boss knows him. Alan Fitch, right?"

"I've heard of Clive Greene," said Tracy. There was the beginning of an annoyed tone creeping into her voice. This wasn't what she had expected.

"Whoa, slow down, Agent Johnson," said Zeke. "I'm not the one who fabricated a missing dog. I called because I wanted to make the connection legitimate. Besides, I amuse myself."

"Clive Greene, how do I know that name?" asked Tracy, now a bit less annoyed.

"I asked Clive, and he said that his Agency was involved in a private protection detail in Atlanta this year. Apparently, the Vice President was here, as well as a number of foreign dignitaries and businessmen. Mr. Fitch was involved in coordinating some of the security."

"That sounds right," said Tracy. "Last spring."

"Yes," said Zeke. "So when I add all this up, I think you may have come across Mr. Cruz recently. We did, too. Seems to me like we might want to get together and share some information."

CHAPTER 16

Growing up, Zeke had lived with his mom and dad aboard a sail boat named *West Wind*. She was a 52-foot Mandarin motorsailer with a single Cummins diesel engine that slept six comfortably and allowed their family the freedom of movement they craved. Zeke's father had retired after sixteen years at a manufacturing facility in Chicago. "Dad," Zeke had called him. Zeke remembered him as a kind and intelligent man who always seemed to have time for his family.

Zeke's mother was a gentle woman with a kind heart. Although Zeke was an only child, he remembered the many times that his mother would adopt Zeke and his neighborhood friends and help them build a fort out of couch cushions or show them maps that led to buried treasures. The treasures, more often than not, were in the form of warm chocolate chip cookies, and the treasure hunters usually ended up finding them by their distinctive smell.

When Dad was diagnosed at his annual company physical with a thickening of his heart muscle, the doctor gave him a treatment plan. “Basically, Ken,” said Doctor Herman, “you’ll have to avoid any kind of stress. That muscle could tighten up and kill you at any time.”

“How do I avoid stress?” Ken Traynor had asked.

“Well, believe it or not, you can do most anything that you want to do, but you’ll need to avoid doing anything that you don’t want to do. The latter is what causes stress and distress.”

With that diagnosis, Zeke’s Dad retired from the company; and the family of three sold their house in Cicero, moved to Florida and bought the sailboat that became their home. Most of Zeke’s memories of life after the age of eight were acquired aboard the *West Wind*. It was a sloop with a gray mainsail and great lines—a real beauty. They kept it in Boot Key Marina, in Marathon.

Zeke became an accomplished first mate and ultimately a proficient sail boat captain aboard the *West Wind*. It wasn’t unusual for the Traynor family to lift anchor and head northwest into the calm waters of the Florida Bay for a few weeks or a month at a time.

The Florida Bay had a calming effect on the whole family, and as often as was practical, they would venture north from Marathon, across the Florida Bay toward the mainland. They would then usually head northwest with the coast in sight on their starboard side, toward the Ten Thousand Islands and Everglades City, careful to avoid the myriad mangrove clusters that were forming new islands in the bay.

The marina that they called home hosted a number of interesting characters, and most of them befriended the young blond boy. They were a diverse group.

There was a Brit and his wife, both in their eighties, and the husband claimed to have been a Rear Admiral in Her Majesty's Navy. The folks in the marina called him Admiral, and he single-handedly tended the massive and colorful flower garden between the marina entrance and his double wide trailer overlooking the piers. His wife, Maude, was a kind lady who always had carmel candies available in a bowl near the front door.

Scooter, the assistant dockmaster, lived aboard a small trawler that had been dry-docked for as long as Zeke could remember. When he wasn't working in the dock office, he was usually working on the hull or the brightwork of his trawler, the *Lazy Jane*. Scooter was small and agile and bounced around the dock area with no apparent effort, pumping fuel or getting beer and ice for visitors and residents alike. The information Scooter shared was often a little bit wrong, but his smile and willingness to help made up for it. Scooter was fascinating to young Zeke, partly because he had lost the last two fingers on his left hand in a boating accident.

"Hey, Zeke," Scooter said one day, as Zeke stopped in to buy some live bait. "How'd you like to meet a Kung Fu expert?"

"Sure," said Zeke. To a young boy, Kung Fu was the rage during the 1980s.

"He just moored that 32-foot live-aboard on Pier 3, Slip 8 there. The *Ryūha*. Watch for him. He's about my height, and he looks Japanese or Korean or something. He looks sort of like a used-camera salesman."

Cool, thought Zeke. He leaned his fishing rod against the

dock office and started toward Pier 3 to check it out. The *Ryūha* was a single-masted sailboat with sleek lines and a minimalistic look. Unusual for that time, the mainsail was a chocolate brown color, with white trim piping. The majority of the exposed surface of the boat was teak, which was well oiled. The bright-work was clean and reflected the Florida sun.

Zeke approached the *Ryūha* and stood on the pier by her slip. He was fascinated by the large oriental character on the slack mainsail.

"Hello, son," said a deep voice in unaccented English. "How do you like her?"

"She's a beauty," said Zeke, admiring the vessel. "Where was your last port?" He didn't see the man, but he assumed that he was speaking from inside the salon.

"I just arrived from Grand Turk," said the voice. It seemed to drift out from an open window on the near side, the port side of the boat. "Before that, it was Aruba."

The man stepped up the interior ladder and out onto the deck near the cockpit and wheel. He was an average sized man, and to Zeke he did indeed look like an oriental camera sales-man. He moved efficiently and effortlessly, although to Zeke he looked to be near fifty years old, certainly older than Zeke's Dad.

"Hello," he said. "My name is Eddie." He held his hand out to Zeke, who took it and shook it from the pier. "I'm Zeke."

"Are you visiting, Zeke?" asked Eddie.

"No, we live just over there." Zeke pointed to the *West Wind*, moored two piers away.

"Aha," said Eddie.

"What does that character on your mainsail mean?" asked Zeke.

"It means Tranquility," said Eddie.

"I thought it might be the symbol for *Ryūha*, the name of your sailboat," said Zeke.

"Ah, no. Ryūha is a school, like a 'school of thought,'" said Eddie. He smiled at Zeke. "Japanese martial arts are classified into ryūha."

"So, are you a Kung Fu expert?" asked the boy.

"No," said Eddie, "that's pretty violent. But I do know a little something about Jiu Jitsu."

"What's that?" asked Zeke.

"Well," said Eddie, "it's also a martial art, but it's all about using your opponent's force and momentum against him rather than meeting force with force."

"Really?" said Zeke. "That sounds pretty cool."

"It is," said Eddie. "The Japanese developed it to fight the samurai years ago."

"Could I learn it?" asked Zeke.

"I'm sure you could," said Eddie. "Anyone can. It starts with the right mindset. Hence, tranquility."

CHAPTER 17

George, The Accountant, was dialing a phone number that rang exactly 2,000 miles away, in a heavily protected villa in San Luis del Colorado, Sonora, Mexico. It was, actually, the largest villa in Sonora, George reflected, and calling it a villa didn't do it justice. It was a castle, perhaps, but not a villa. The phone George was calling from was a pre-paid cell phone, and he had disabled its GPS tracking to make it untraceable.

The next step would be to re-establish contact with Cruz and make new arrangements to recover the stolen money and the plates. George was fairly certain that this time Jefe would expect that Cruz be eliminated at the drop point as collateral damage. There was too much risk, in George's mind, to let him live. Already the Secret Service was involved, and no one could afford the trouble they could bring if they were pointed in the right direction. No, Cruz was a dead man walking, as was his immediate family in Sonora Rio. Someone else, someone local to them, would take care of that.

He heard the distant ringing, and after four rings Jefe

answered. *Perhaps he had been playing with the bambinos,* George thought.

"Si," said Jefe.

"Excuse me, Jefe," said George. "I am calling to report."

"Si," said Jefe.

Continuing in Spanish, George outlined the activity at the coffee shop Friday evening. Cruz had not come, as promised, but had sent a man who resembled him to make the transfer. George had initiated action against the man, initially thought to be Cruz, but someone else had intervened and taken the backpack with the money and the printer plates. George had followed him and isolated the man's activity to three buildings. Outside of the third building, he, George, had retrieved the man's backpack, but found it to be empty.

"What do you suggest that we do?" asked Jefe. This was a dangerous question, in that it set George up as responsible for any future failures in his plan.

"Jefe, I will find Alberto Cruz and retrieve your belongings," said George, because he knew that no other answer would be acceptable.

"Si," said Jefe.

* * *

"I don't care what it takes," Fitch was saying, "You've got to find this guy."

It was Saturday afternoon, and Tracy Johnson and Ron Marcus were sitting in one of the small conference rooms and briefing their boss on the current status of the manhunt. Through the window, the outside view of the Atlanta skyline was deceptively calm. Fitch was anything but calm.

Alan Fitch had been with the Secret Service for over twenty-five years, and had risen quickly to supervisory positions. His service record was stellar, and in his annual reviews he typically rated in the top ten percent of the agents. Fitch was active in Personal Protection Details in his early career, both because of his physical prowess and his intense focus and commitment.

At six feet five inches tall, Fitch began his work in the Personal Protection Detail, and within eight years had attained the prestigious position as one of the "human wall" that surrounds the President of the United States in times of trouble. His career in this position spanned three Presidents.

Then, in May 2005, President George W. Bush was giving a speech in the Freedom Square in Tbilisi, Georgia, a part of the former Soviet Union, when a live RDG-5 Soviet hand grenade was thrown at the podium from which he was speaking. Unfortunately, Fitch had been on duty that day, and although the grenade did not detonate, the political shrapnel was enough to derail his career. He was moved to Atlanta shortly thereafter.

Today, Fitch was angry. His face was red as he paced the small room.

Tracy noticed that the active pronoun had shifted from first person plural to second person plural, from "we" to "you", as in, "You've got to find this guy." *There's no "I" in "team"*, she thought. *And there's no Fitch in "team" either.*

Setting up a perimeter would have been impossible, considering that the time of the hit-and-run was 4:50 PM on a Friday evening, almost exactly the time that most of the office buildings in downtown Atlanta, a city of almost a half million people, called it a day. Traffic north and south along the Interstates would be bumper to bumper, and there were just too many alternative routes out of the city for the Georgia Highway Patrol to cover.

A door-to-door search had been considered, but the idea was dismissed due to the transient nature of the neighborhood, the students and the downtown activity. Officers were stationed at Cruz's hotel, both in the lobby and in the corridor to his room. His cell phone GPS was being actively tracked (it appeared that the phone was off), and BOLO's had been sent to all the rental car agencies, the airport and TSA, the bus terminals, taxi cabs, the Amtrak personnel, MARTA police and, because of the proximity, the Georgia Tech campus police. A few younger sheriffs' deputies in plain clothes were circulating around the campus, stopping in shops and restaurants and watching for the illusive Mexican. And watching for the missing printer plates.

Further, if Cruz used any of his credit or debit cards, red flags would fly, and Tracy's office would be notified. If he turned his cell phone on, they would be alerted immediately. If he bought a ticket, rented a car or hotel room, took a cab or grabbed some dinner, the Secret Service would know.

That's how Tracy had spent her Saturday. Since then, almost 24 hours from his no-show at the coffee shop, the Secret Service offices had been commandeered and were being used as a com center, a clearing house for any and all information and coordination in finding this critical target. At the same time, everything Cruz was being re-looked, re-thought and reviewed by an independent team of agents from outside the original operation. They had arrived this morning from D.C and had spent the day sifting back through every note, every conversation, every videotape, and every communication that had taken place with or about Cruz. Two of the team had been assigned as deep background researchers, looking specifically at Cruz's habits and history.

We've got to catch a break, Tracy thought. *Something has to happen.* Tracy figured that Fitch was upset because he'd let the counterfeiting plates go and was bound to lose face if they weren't returned. It would be his second strike. Maybe not career ending, but certainly uncomfortable and embarrassing. *Sort of along the lines of losing his weapon to a perp*, she thought. But it didn't reflect well on her either, she admitted to herself.

"So, boss, do you think Cruz insisted on having the original printer plates at the exchange for credibility, or do you think he planned this all along?" asked Ron, who was sitting across from Tracy.

"It doesn't matter," said Fitch. "What matters is that we find him and the plates and get it all back here where they belong." Cruz had been very convincing as he described Jefe's operation and the need for "authentic equipment" at the exchange.

"I'll be back in a minute," said Fitch, and he left the conference room with a scowl on his face.

"So, we know that Cruz worked for Jefe in his counterfeiting operation," said Ron. "And we know that he's been there for a long time, years. So then, all of a sudden, Cruz decides to leave town on the run. Why?"

"He could have been in danger in Mexico," Tracy said. "Or maybe he crossed Jefe somehow. He could have been skimming off the top, and was caught."

"So, for whatever reason, Cruz gets in his car and drives to Phoenix, and then he flies to Atlanta to escape. But somebody spots him leaving, and when he gets here, he realizes that he hasn't escaped at all. They watch him and they make it clear that he's on borrowed time."

"Sounds right so far," said Tracy, and she nodded. She noticed that it was after five o'clock, and as she glanced around she realized that no one in the office was even thinking about going home yet.

"And," continued Ron, "Cruz took printer plates and several hundred thousand dollars worth of counterfeit money with him."

"Maybe more than that," said Tracy. "We don't know what he might have held back."

"Right," said Ron. He thought some more.

"So, Mr. Cruz is renting a house not far from here when he realizes that he's caught, he's been found out," Ron continued. "The tough guys are coming to town, and Cruz is no fighter. He's an artist."

"Yep," Tracy nodded again. "So he runs for the closest help he can find, the police."

"Who basically tell him they won't babysit him, that no

crime has been committed, and that there's nothing they can do. When he mentions counterfeiting, they tell him he needs to talk with us."

"Right," said Tracy, "and since he's on a limited time visa, and since there's the counterfeiting crime involved, the political brass decides that they should pawn this off on the Feds. It's too volatile to ignore, and they don't need any bad press that comes from the situation. The easy move is to wrap Cruz up and deliver him here, to the 'counterfeiting specialists'. That would be us."

"So the week he was here, he spent every minute in this office with some of us," said Ron. "We thought we were keeping him close to keep an eye on him, but Mr. Cruz was staying here for his own protection. Clever man. He even agreed to sleep here the first nights, when Fitch brought it up."

Tracy nodded. She was wearing a green cable sweater, an Irish looking color, over boot-cut jeans and black ankle boots. Her brown shoulder length hair was worn down today, framing her features, and her makeup was minimal.

"So," she said, "The arrangement to return the printer plates, the exchange, Cruz ran on his own game plan there, too."

"He did. He found a substitute to meet with Jefe's man, knowing that there was a good case for his demise at that point. I'm sure he had an idea that the substitute might end up dead," said Ron.

"Maybe, but it will be tough to prove it," Tracy said.

"And Mr. Cruz is a magician. While we were all watching the diversion, he made himself disappear."

Chapter 18

Alberto Cruz was very careful. Especially now that he'd escaped a potentially deadly trap and had essentially disappeared from sight. Being an artist, and a careful and cautious one at that, Cruz knew how to first visualize the end result and then bring the small supporting components – the brush strokes – into play. He understood deception. Cruz had long been a survivor.

Cruz was nothing if not cautious. As an artist, he was predisposed to slow, painstaking detail and extensive preparation. He had once spent 56 and a half hours copying the detail of Benjamin Franklin's face from a US $100 bill, only to discard the results and start over. He was a perfectionist; that was certain.

For years, Cruz had avoided being on the cartel's radar screen, working behind the scenes on smaller and less valuable forgeries. He had settled for less in order to avoid being visible, a position that, as he had known instinctively, he would lose both control and freedom. Although he acted simple and at times ignorant, and although he looked short and squat and disheveled, Cruz was a man of extraordinary intelligence and craftiness. He combined street smarts with a unique cleverness that his appearance belied.

Growing up in San Luis Rio Colorado, or Sonora Rio, as the locals called it, was difficult. It called for a level of guile, of invisibility, of deception. During the summers this was the hottest place in Mexico...and one of the hottest places in the world. In the summer months, the temperature ranged between 77 degrees and 113 degrees Fahrenheit, with the desert dryness being the only saving factor. Cruz remembered the debilitating heat and the afternoon searches for shade and breeze. The latter was an unusual meteorological occurrence, usually preceding the occasional summer storm.

As a child, Alberto had developed slowly. In his early years, adopted by an aunt, Tia Romana, he had been round and overweight and introverted. He had been bullied mercilessly in school and had ultimately dropped out of the High School on Calle 31 to avoid the constant abuse. At fourteen, Alberto had moved south to work with his dead mother's brother, his uncle, in the port town of Puerto Peñasco, the Rocky Point. Uncle Pablo was a fisherman, a proud man who supported his family and extended family through hard work and meager living. And through some shady activities.

Uncle Pablo had acquired a boat, El Barco, a few years before Alberto moved to the port city. It was a solid fishing boat, with rusty-but-working cable arms for traps and large rigs for netting fish and shrimp. Alberto came aboard as a teenager and spent the next four years working with his uncle. Eventually, there was nothing aboard the boat that he wasn't able to do, from mending the nets with the other men, to repairing the engine, to scaling and cooking the fish for lunch or dinner.

In what little spare time he had, Alberto read and learned. He ingested any books that he could find, reading them many times, books in both Spanish and English, books new and old, from whatever the source. He never tired of the Puerto Peñasco Public Library, and visited there whenever he was off the boat.

The Puerto Peñasco Public Library is where Alberto met his wife. At seventeen, he had grown leaner and, although still short and barrel chested, like many young men he had acquired an air of confidence. He returned a book at the counter, and as he pushed open the library door to leave he saw a beautiful young woman approaching from the parking lot. He paused and held the door open until she arrived.

From his perspective, she looked to be eighteen or twenty years old, with long black hair and dark eyes set in a soft round face. Her hair was pulled back and tied in a small scarf with Indian patterns on it, and her look was a serious one. She was wearing a cotton dress that matched the scarf and fell to just below her knees. Her shoes were black with a single strap.

Cruz immediately looked around for her chaperone, probably her mother or an aunt. It was unusual for young, single Mexican girls to travel alone in Puerto Peñasco. But he saw no one else.

"Excuse me, ma'am," Cruz said in Spanish, still holding the library door open, "Your look is so serious...can I help you?"

"Oh, no, thank you, senor," she said. Her unexpected accent caused him to rethink her origins, and he was now leaning more toward South America, perhaps Ecuador.

"You aren't from around here, are you?" he asked politely as she passed through the door he held.

"Thank you," she stopped and looked back at him, "for holding the door, I mean." She was deciding something, he could tell.

"De Nada," he said. "You're sure I can't help?"

"Well," and then she made her decision. It didn't hurt that Cruz had grown into a strong, good looking young man while working on his uncle's boat. "Well, my car has stopped, and I was able to get it into the library parking lot, but no farther. I was going to ask the librarians for help, or to call someone."

"I'm very good with engines," Cruz said. "Let's take a look at it."

"Thank you," she said. "I am Graciela," she added.

"I am Alberto," he responded.

* * *

Over time, Cruz's language skills grew and by watching shows on U.S. television, Alberto was able to lose his accent. By then, he was both crafty and instinctive, characteristics he had learned from Uncle Pablo and from his time on the streets of Puerto Peñasco.

"Tonight we'll make another run out to the freighter and bring in some square grouper," said Uncle Pablo. "We can take Raul and Franco with us; it shouldn't take more than three or four hours each way with these calm seas."

The freighters would come as far north as the Isla Angel de la Garda, Archangel Island, and would wait there, offshore and concealed in the dark. They ran with no running lights and were skittishly ready to disappear at any moment. Those ships had been fitted with stationary machine guns, fore and aft.

"OK," said Alberto, "I'll pack the bait coolers." Typically, the crew on El Barco would fish on the way out to meet the Colombian freighter in international waters, then wait in line to load bales of marijuana wrapped in black garbage bags onto the fishing boats. If they caught fish - usually Mahi Mahi or Yellow Fin Snapper - they counted the trip as a double success. Uncle Pablo was a thrifty, practical man.

The Colombian freighters would leave from Port of Buenaventura near Cali, and speedboats would rush out to meet them as they made their way north along the Colombian border and passed by Panama. Loaded with the bales, they would then cruise north in the Pacific Ocean, up the Gulf of California, and meet the local fishing boats in an isolated area off the Baja Peninsula. Then, in the dark of night and weighed down with as much as they could carry, the small boats would make their way back to their northern port.

Occasionally, Cruz noted, greed would cause a captain to overload his fishing boat; and in rough seas, that could be fatal. Most of the time, though, the shipments arrived without incident. The fishermen were paid for their delivery, and the bales were loaded onto an eighteen-wheeler and driven to their final destination. The rumor was that these shipments were transported across the border into the United States, but Cruz didn't know how. Perhaps by small plane or tunnel, he imagined. Or maybe corrupt border guards.

Alberto was still a teenager when he started noticing the changes in Puerto Peñasco.

"Arturo," Cruz said to a friend who crewed on the fishing boat that docked next to his Uncle's boat in the City Marina. "I noticed that your father is driving a new car."

"Yes, he saw that some of the other fishermen had traded their old trucks in, and it gave him the idea," said Arturo. "How do you like it? We're riding in style now! And with air conditioning that works!"

The car was a brand new, powder blue 1984 Cadillac Coupe de Ville and would have looked out of place parked in the marina lot a few years ago. The vehicles typical to that area were old pickup trucks, small mopeds and older compact cars, rusted by the salt air. They were, for the most part, work vehicles that were well used and looked it.

But that was a few years ago. Today, the new Cadillac was surrounded by luxurious automobiles, Lincoln Town cars and Mercedes Benz, among others.

Not much later, some of the fishermen bought new fishing boats, and a few of them bought two or three vessels, to leverage their profits. Alberto's Uncle was angry.

"Look at this," he said to Alberto, waving his arm toward the marina and the parking lot. "This is like advertising, saying, 'We're running drugs!' They will get us all in trouble!"

Predictably, not long after this the Puerto Peñasco Police, with the cooperation of the US DEA, raided the Puerto Peñasco

City Marina. By that time, almost every family in the town was involved in the enterprise in some way. Just about every adult male went to jail, including Alberto's Uncle. And all of the new boats and cars were confiscated by the Puerto Peñasco police.

Alberto, now without means to earn money, found himself heading back to Sonora Rio. There he found work, first as a day laborer, and later as an auto mechanic, using the skills he had learned aboard his Uncle's boat. After a few months, when he had earned enough, he drove his second-hand Volkswagen Beetle back to Puerto Peñasco each weekend to visit Graciela.

Chapter 19

Finding Cruz had been a huge win for Tracy and her team. They'd seen it as the possible beginning of a major operation, one that could make a serious impact on the flow of counterfeit money into the United States. They were all anxious; they all wanted this to work. And they all were leaning in just a bit too much, wanting it, needing it. Careers were made from this type of operation.

During their time together, Cruz had emphasized the language differences and used them to break the flow of the interviews. He was seemingly confused by wording, or misunderstood questions, not to the point that a translator was needed, but enough that he had time to gather his thoughts and undermine the rhythm that the interviewer was trying to establish. Occasionally, he would misunderstand a question or the intent behind it. But after a couple of days, the agents relaxed.

And during these days, Cruz remembered everything he saw. His life depended on it. He heard the agents on their personal calls, he knew who had children in school, who was ambitious and who was complacent. He found out who was married and who lived alone; and he memorized telephone numbers and passwords from watching the agents type on keypads on their phones and computers.

In the Atlanta Field Office of the Secret Service on Spring Street, Cruz was an unusual visitor. Typically, witnesses taken there were interviewed and then turned loose to return home or to work. The offices didn't really have a place to detain people, and suspects were usually taken to a different location, one with detention capabilities. But, because of the threat on Cruz's life, the agents had secreted him in this office location. And it was not really set up or equipped for the retention of criminals. It was more an operational facility than a tactical one.

Consequently, the standard positioning with the interviewer on one side of the table and the interviewee on the other - normal questioning techniques in law enforcement - wasn't possible. Instead, Cruz was interviewed either sitting next to an agent's desk, in a small conference room, or in a sitting area in the interior hallway, furnished like a small waiting area in a typical hospital. And Cruz was often left waiting, while the agents he was working with attended meetings, or took phone calls, or filled out forms and reports, or talked with their bosses.

As the week progressed, Cruz became more and more invisible to the agents. Everyone knew that he was there because his life had been threatened. And everyone knew that he was under the charge of Tracy and Ron. So, most of the agents began to dismiss his presence, and he became more and more invisible. Agents talked on their phones in his presence, talked with each other about other cases in his presence, asked each other questions and devised strategies. Cruz spent his time filing away many small pieces of information.

By not playing the victim, and handling himself with a bearing that implied equality, Cruz was able to gain a position of semi-trust among some of the agents. He gave a polite distance and kept to himself, but without any attitude or fear.

* * *

The money is the next problem, thought Zeke. It was 10:30 on Saturday morning, and Zeke had spent most of the night awake, reviewing Friday's events, and constructing likely scenarios of the motivating forces. Many things fit into place, but the money and the printer plates were still the problem. They were most likely safe for the weekend, and perhaps longer, but any number of things could go wrong. They could be discovered by the way the ceiling tiles bulged a bit. Or a random electrical repair - say a fluorescent fixture ballast or bulb replacement - would likely result in them being noticed. Or a footprint on a chair might cause the inquisitive office worker to look up, and to start thinking.

So, retrieving the hidden items was the next priority. Zeke liked the Student Union lockers as a secure, temporary place to keep it all. But getting them there would be the riskiest part of this operation so far.

The Accountant, George, was in Atlanta. And he knew about the money and the plates, and now he knew about Zeke. He was hunting, Zeke was sure, and he would stay focused on the campus, the area where he'd seen Zeke before.

The library was open every day including Saturday, although weekend hours were a bit more restrictive than weekdays. The library opened later, at noon on Saturday, and closed earlier, at 5:00 PM. Zeke looked at his watch, did a quick calculation, and decided that a short nap would be the best way to fill the interim hour and fifteen minutes.

CHAPTER 20

Cruz was watching for George. He was expecting that devil to show up at any moment, without warning. Jefe's men were watching Cruz, and they had left him nowhere to run. But when the meeting took place, it didn't happen the way he'd expected.

Alberto had been lying low, hiding in his rented house in south Fulton County. He'd chosen that neighborhood because it was a short, direct drive to the airport, and even in traffic he could be there in 30 minutes or less. It was a small bungalow, one-story, brick ranch, in a tract neighborhood on a street populated by a rail worker, a mailman, an auto mechanic, a disabled guy, a bus driver for MARTA and several working single mothers. He wasn't really sure what the mothers did... maybe some government jobs, or possibly they worked for a utility company.

The restaurant on the corner was adequate. El Toro, it was called. The food wasn't really Mexican, but the portions were large, and he could blend in there, not stand out much. For lunch each day Cruz would go to either El Toro or, in the other direction to a fried chicken restaurant, a local place that served the chicken dripping with grease, along with sides of biscuits and fried okra. Sitting at his kitchen table at eleven-thirty that Saturday morning, Cruz thought about his options. Then he stood, picked up his hat, and walked out the front door, turning left toward El Toro.

As he walked toward the restaurant he was feeling a bit exposed. He took a seat in El Toro, a small diner-type restaurant, in a booth with high-backed vinyl bench seats and a patterned Formica tabletop. He had ordered at the counter and was eating a plate of black beans and rice when suddenly two men sat down with him.

One took the bench across from Cruz, and the second slid in next to him, effectively blocking him into the booth. The movement was abrupt and rough, and the second man ended up pressed against Cruz's thigh. Cruz moved uncomfortably toward the window a bit, creating a small space between himself and the man. He looked up at them.

What he saw was two Hispanic men in their early thirties, not fat, not thin, with yuppie haircuts and designer jeans. He saw two open-necked dress shirts and no t-shirts, just black chest hair. He saw open faces and four brown eyes, looking at him. He thought, *Mierda,* but his eyes showed nothing but a question.

"Hello, Alberto," said the man next to him. The men spoke in Spanish, Mexican Spanish.

"Do I know you?" Cruz asked.

"Jefe sent us to visit with you," the man continued. "I'm

Ricardo, and my friend here is Umberto. You have something that belongs to Jefe, we believe," said Ricardo. "Something he values."

Cruz's stomach froze and then sank a bit. He spoke his fear. "Are you here to kill me?" he asked.

The men glanced at each other and smiled, an inside joke, apparently. "No, Alberto, we're not rough guys. We're the guys Jefe sends out first, to negotiate, to recover his property, to set things right. We're sort of like management consultants. They find out about a problem in the organization, and we're sent out to fix it. Troubleshooters. Usually, that takes discussion, maybe negotiation, or maybe some retraining. Like that. We try to look for a mutually acceptable solution to these problems," said Ricardo, "to keep the business productive and the money flowing. Umberto and I, we both have MBA's."

Cruz didn't believe them, so he smiled absently.

"And, if we can't fix the problem, Alberto, then they send out a different man. And he's the one you would be worried about." This from Ricardo. "Think of how expensive it would be to send that guy, the Accountant, out to solve every little problem. It might damage the organization unnecessarily, too. He's not so much about discussions and negotiations and training, you know? He is heavier handed. They call him the Accountant because it's his job to erase the liabilities. So you see, we're like the advance scouts, the first wave, your chance to bring this thing to a more civilized and reasonable conclusion."

Cruz took a mouthful of beans and rice, filling his mouth to stall for time. He was thinking.

He swallowed.

"Yes, I see," he said. "That makes good sense. Why waste resources, right?" He smiled again, pretty certain that nothing would happen in the crowded restaurant. He was in no hurry to leave the premises. "What can I do to help you, my friends?"

Ricardo continued. He was obviously the chatty one. Or, perhaps he spoke better English than Umberto. Oddly, they had shifted to speaking in English. "As I said, you have something that belongs to Jefe, something that he values and that he wants back." He stopped talking and just stared at Alberto, waiting for a response. No blinking, no looking away, just a wide-eyed stare, the expectation of an explanation.

"You mean the printer plates, I presume," Cruz said. Alberto looked up at the men, and then moved his head a bit to his right. "I think we may have a common problem, my friends," he said. "I have also been the victim of theft. I'm glad you're here to help me find and return these items." He put his forefinger on his lips to stop himself from talking more and looked back at Ricardo.

"Who took them?" asked Umberto. His first words.

"It was someone at the hotel," lied Cruz. "When I first arrived here, I stayed in a hotel downtown for a few days. While I was out, my suitcase with the counterfeit plates in it was stolen. I haven't been able to find it. I don't know what to do." Cruz pouted a bit and took a final bite of his food. And he swallowed again.

Umberto looked at Ricardo. Ricardo glanced at him, and then looked back at Cruz.

"Oh, this is not good, amigo," he said, and shook his head.

"My friends, I will help in any way that I can," said Cruz. He looked at each of the men, but neither was smiling.

They seemed to realize that they had reached an impasse in this crowded place. Their message delivered, along with the non-verbal "We can find you whenever we wish," Umberto and Ricardo glanced at each other and stood simultaneously.

"I suggest that you make an effort to contact those with Jefe's money and printer plates, and retrieve them. We'll come by your house in a day or two, and we can discuss your progress then." Umberto said this with an air of certainty, as if there would be no trouble finding Cruz at any time, and there was no question of his cooperation.

"Si, yes, of course," Cruz said.

Cruz remembered the meeting as if it had taken place yesterday. But it had been six days ago. After that encounter, Cruz immediately hired Clive and The Agency to protect him from Jefe's men.

CHAPTER 21

The second time that Zeke met Tracy Johnson face-to-face she was wearing tight, cuffed jeans, low-cut boots and a loose, red sweater. Her dark, thick hair was again pulled back from her face into an organized, full ponytail, and her understated makeup still did little to emphasize her outstanding features. She was sitting in a brown leather wingback chair in the lobby of the Embassy Suites Hotel, across from the front desk. There was a second, identical chair across from her, and a small glass coffee table between them.

Zeke dropped into the second chair, looked at her for a moment and said, "Hello, Tracy Johnson."

"Hello, yourself," she said, as she looked over at him. Her smile implied that this might be more than a business meeting. "You surprised me with your phone call."

"You should be used to getting calls from available young men," Zeke teased.

"Why do you say that?" she asked.

"No wedding ring," he continued. "It's obvious that you take care of yourself. You dress well, have good posture, and you seem competent and intelligent," he continued. "School?"

"Wharton," she said.

"So, competent and very intelligent. Are you in a relationship?"

"Just with my job this month," Tracy sighed.

"I'm guessing that you're not long alone, maybe out of a relationship within the last six weeks."

"Why do you guess that?" she asked.

"And probably a workplace romance," he continued.

"Probably," echoed Tracy.

"Not my business, I suppose," said Zeke. "I'm more interested in your future than in your past."

"Nicely said." Tracy paused. "Can we chat about Cruz now?"

"That's why we're here, isn't it?" asked Zeke.

* * *

"I did have some questions for you," said Tracy after they had traded information about Alberto Cruz. "I have to admit, I Googled you before this meeting."

Zeke had been careful, revealing only information about his client that Tracy already knew, or that could be obtained from public sources. "There's no hiding from the Internet," he said.

"You were in Sydney in the 2002 Olympics. Were you on the Judo Team?"

"As an alternate. I spent most of my time on the practice squad, getting bounced around by the really good guys."

"How did you get into that sport?" she asked. She gave him her full attention, leaned forward to hear his answer and looked at him directly with wide-open eyes. *He has great eyes,* she thought.

She's flirting, he thought. *Nice.*

"I blame Eddie for that," Zeke said, smiling again.

"Eddie?"

"Eddie was a fellow I met when I was a boy, the man who brought me up after my parents died." He paused for a second. "He was in the military, stationed in Japan originally, and he also studied Judo in Okinawa."

"Your parents died?"

"It was a boating accident. I lost them both when a fuel tank exploded on our motorsailer. I'd gone ashore to buy a Coke and heard and felt the explosion from the little store. That's a long time ago," he added.

"I'm sorry," she said.

"So Eddie took me in, and over the years he taught me Judo and Jiu-jitsu. He was really quick and tough, and I guess he was a good teacher, because the next thing I knew I was practicing in Colorado Springs."

"What's there?"

"The U.S. Olympic training facility," Zeke said. "Hey, let's grab some lunch."

"OK," Tracy said.

* * *

The hotel Bistro was pretty much empty and the shift had apparently just changed, Zeke noticed. The bartender was busy checking inventory and the server looked alert and fresh, her hair still neatly arranged and her clothing without a wrinkle or stain. *She smells a bit like fresh cut cilantro and lime,* Zeke thought as she approached.

"Would you like to start with a drink?" the server asked.

"Tracy?" asked Zeke.

"May I have unsweetened tea?" she asked the server.

"Yes, ma'am. And you, sir?"

"Water with lemon, please," said Zeke. He remembered recently reading a quote that lemons are 'packed like a clown car' with a variety of vitamins and nutrients. In a quick moment, he itemized them all in his mind.

"What are you thinking about?" asked Tracy, once the server left.

"Just amusing myself," said Zeke, and he smiled. "You're an only child."

"I am. How would you know that?" asked Tracy.

"It's what I do," said Zeke.

"As I said, I researched you before I came here, and I talked with Fitch about you," said Tracy, looking away for a moment, then back at Zeke.

The server came back with their drinks and took their food order.

"What did you find about me?" asked Zeke, when they were alone again.

"Well, in addition to the aptitude you have for some of the

martial arts, I saw that you worked as a contractor for Army Intelligence. You were in Iraq and a few other pretty volatile places. From the sound of it, I'd guess you were an operative. At least a part of the intelligence community."

"I can't really talk about that," said Zeke.

"Fitch said that Clive Greene was a consultant to MICECP for a while."

Zeke smiled at her. "I heard something like that, too," he said.

"You said your Judo instructor adopted you?"

"Sort of. It wasn't formal, but he took good care of me after my folks passed away. Watched out for me and kept me out of trouble."

"Where did you live?"

"In a marina in the Keys. After our boat exploded, I moved in with a couple that lived aboard a 57-foot Chris Craft Constellation. I was pretty young, and most people down there were like family. So I was able to continue my homeschooling, and I practiced Judo with Eddie most days," Zeke said. "They say it takes a village, but in my case, it took a marina."

"But, honestly, Tracy," Zeke said with a smile, "I'd rather talk about you."

CHAPTER 22

"It's all in a locker at the Student Union. Here's the key."

Zeke and Clive were in line in the coffee shop while waiting for the barista to finish their orders. It was Saturday afternoon, and the place was filling up with students whose hair looked like they'd slept in late. Some had, some hadn't.

"All right," said Clive. "I'll have someone gather it up and be sure to get it in the Secret Service's hands. Say we found it or something."

"Alright, thanks, Clive. I think they'll be glad to have it back, quite honestly. Their operation was a mess."

"They will most likely," said Clive, "but they probably won't say so."

The barista called his name, and Clive stepped forward and took the paper cup in his hand. He smelled the contents. "Ah, Earl Grey," he said.

Zeke could smell the citrus odor wafting from the uncovered cup of tea.

"That bergamot orange is carcinogenic, you know," said Zeke.

Clive looked at Zeke as if he'd spoken in Kiswahili. "Any word from Cruz?" asked Clive, changing the subject.

"No, I haven't heard a word from him since I found him in my apartment last evening. We talked, and he left. Didn't say where he was going. He said he'd be back, but he never showed up."

"We can't protect someone we can't find," said Clive. "He could be out there, exposed, or he could have taken off. But we can't protect him if he won't work with us, right?"

"Right." Zeke's name was called, and he turned and grabbed his coffee. "I think he'll show up when he needs us again. Let's see about finding George, the Accountant since we have a little time. If we neutralize George as a threat, Cruz should be safe for a while."

"That's what we're being paid to do," said Clive.

They moved to a small, round, blond wooden table and sat on two upholstered chairs near the front window, away from other patrons. It was September and the flowers were still colorful in the beds on the other side of the glass. Purples, yellows and light greens prevailed, low and bright against the contrasting brick in the afternoon sun.

"OK, let's figure this out. What do we know about the Accountant?" Clive asked.

"From Cruz, we know that he was seen around the coffee shop, here, Friday mid-afternoon. I saw him on the street, just there, about 5 o'clock Friday. After that, I saw him in the campus library. He gained access pretty quickly, so he must have had a student or faculty ID of some kind. He would have had to stop and sign in if he'd had a visitor's pass. My guess is he's familiar with the campus and has arranged access in advance. So he's thorough. And, based on his knowledge of the area, he's staying nearby, maybe even on campus."

Clive nodded. "What else do we have?" It was a game they played, thinking out loud, building on each other's insights, following the rhythm of the words.

"Well," Zeke continued, "when I left the library, he followed me to the Engineering Building. But I didn't see him most of the time. Which means that he has skills."

"Right, I'd expect no less," said Clive.

"And, apparently, he chose the backpack over me, after I threw it in the garbage. Which means that he couldn't take the chance that the backpack wasn't empty. He had to check."

"Or, he already knows how to find you, so the backpack was of a higher interest to him," Clive thought out loud.

"He's been on foot every time I've seen him," Zeke continued. "He may not have a car here, or he may choose to leave it garaged, which means that he might be staying close by, within an easy walk."

"Right," Clive agreed. "Not many places to park on campus unless you have a permit. He could have arranged for one, but having a vehicle on campus can be cumbersome. And the public parking around here is very limited. There's street parking, which you can't count on, and the Peters Parking Deck, which stays full most weekdays."

"And he had to be just a short walk from the coffee shop, for a quick escape once he had the bag."

"So, the hotel option, then," said Clive. "Again, he'd probably need to be close by the campus and the coffee shop, for the critical minutes when he leaves with the backpack."

"Right, and it's unlikely that he'd cross Interstate 85 on foot, even with the overpasses and sidewalks. It's very exposed and is about a half mile away. What if it had been raining?"

"OK, so the obvious choice is the Hampton Inn, a block south of the campus. Wait," Zeke said. He thought. "OK, so that's not it. He'll be at the second or third closest hotel. He'd risk the weather."

"Why do you think that," Clive asked.

"He's too memorable. All we'd have to do is talk with the folks at the front desk and ask if they have any very short guests. He'd be busted."

"That's true, Zeke. So, walking distance?"

"Most likely the Hyatt House, the Hilton Garden Inn or the Embassy Suites, I'd say. Possibly he's at the Omni. South of the campus, south of my apartment, and on the same side of the Interstate."

"OK, which one?" said Clive.

"I'd bet on the Omni. It's at CNN Center, which is a very busy place. The hotel has over a thousand rooms, so it would be easy to lose yourself in the complex. And it's a four-star hotel. Our guy picks four-star hotels whenever he can. He thinks he deserves it," said Zeke. "Icing?"

"OK, Icing," said Clive.

"The Omni is less than 30 minutes from the Atlanta Airport, by MARTA transit. And the hotel is just across Centennial Park from the MARTA station for a quick exit. So he doesn't need a car."

Clive said, "And the Omni's a tourist destination, good for staying invisible. Let's go."

CHAPTER 23

Tracy was ignoring Ron's smirk.

"This guy really played you," said Ron.

Tracy looked over at him with a withering look and then looked back at her phone. She was reading the most recent Service e-mail discussing Cruz's whereabouts.

"He's got to be somewhere," she said, mostly to herself. So far, the trail was dead. Cruz hadn't used any credit cards or any ATM's since he disappeared. He hadn't used his cell phone. It was shut off, disabling the GPS chip inside. He hadn't taken a flight, rented a car, eaten a meal or paid for a hotel room, to the best of anyone's knowledge. His absence was disturbing.

"He could be dead," Ron continued. "Perhaps that fellow he told us about, the Accountant, caught up with him. If so, his body will probably turn up in an abandoned car or a hotel room pretty soon."

"Hmm," said Tracy, thinking.

Ron and Tracy were sitting in a black Crown Vic, the Secret Service's vehicle of choice. Ron was in the driver's seat. They were parked in a diagonal parking slot in a retail strip center across from Cruz's house in south Fulton County. If he twisted just right, Ron could see the top edge of the El Toro restaurant sign down at the end of the block. So far, the house had remained empty and quiet.

It was a warm day, so they had the windows up and the engine idling to keep the air conditioning active. They weren't well disguised. An observer would have seen the white exhaust smoke and the two heads in the driver and passenger seats. But so far, there were no observers. The street was quiet just before dinnertime on Saturday. It seemed that everyone in the neighborhood was busy indoors or away, shopping or visiting family perhaps.

A large pit bull in a nearby fenced yard had greeted them with excited barks and growls when they first arrived and parked on the street. When Ron moved the car to the parking lot, the dog came as close as he could, pressing his wide body up against the chain link fence, and then he lay down watching them carefully.

"If Cruz isn't dead," said Ron, "then maybe he's staying with a friend or family member." They had considered that possibility before.

"No way to know," said Tracy. "We don't have enough information to tell whether he has extended family here in Atlanta, but if he does, it would be a perfect place to hole up."

Earlier, a Secret Service agent named Enrique Diaz, on staff in Washington, DC, had researched Cruz's immediate family in Sonora, and had called and asked some members of his family about Cruz's friends or relatives in the United States. He drew a blank. He also contacted the Mexican Police, "Policía Federal". There was no quick help there, either, although it came as no surprise. Most everyone in federal law enforcement knows that Mexico's police have a reputation as one of the more corrupt forces.

"Ah, we would like to help you, senor," said the voice from the Federales offices in Mexico City, "But in Sonora there was a tragedy last year. The police chief, Chief Manny Lopez, was murdered. He was gunned down, shot with AK-47's maybe thirty times. He was off duty and leaving his home when they shot him."

"Has anyone replaced Lopez?" asked Enrique.

"No, no, it is difficult to fill a position that has been vacated so dramatically," said the officer.

"Have the men who shot him been arrested?" Enrique asked, knowing the answer as the words left his lips.

"No, senior. That is the territory of Jefe. Not many wish to be in a position opposing Jefe and his operation. It would not be wise."

"I understand," said Enrique. "Gracias, senior." He hung up the phone and dialed Tracy's cell number.

* * *

In fact, Chief Manny Lopez had been raised by his mother in Sonora Rio before he moved to the United States at age 18 to live and work with his uncle, his mother's sister's husband,

Jorge. Jorge was a large man who owned a tow truck business, and with the help of his two sons and Manny, the business grew.

Like most men in the shadier parts of Yuma, Arizona, Manny quickly learned to avoid trouble and watch out for himself. The streets were difficult, but not as difficult as some areas of Sonora Rio. There were times to ignore what you saw, and times to take advantage. No one was going to give you anything, his cousin Tito told him over and over. No one cares about you. You have to learn to fend for yourself. Anything you need, you have to take it.

More than once, Manny's pay was shorted.

"Uncle Jorge, this is less than I thought it would be," said Manny, looking at his pay envelope.

"Yes, I know, but it was a slow week, and we had to pay to get the truck serviced," Jorge responded. Always with an excuse, Manny seldom received the money he was owed.

"Besides," Uncle Jorge would say, "what are you going to do with the money, anyhow? Just spend it on beer and poker."

Uncle Jorge was well known in Yuma. He named the business after his boys, Pep and Tito, and arranged to handle all of the local police towing needs. Abandoned cars, illegal parking, policing parking lots for abandons and violators were all part of the business. A few years later, Jorge expanded his brand into a parallel line of business, auto repossessions. The young men would spend nights driving around looking for repos to hook up and tow back to the sales lots.

"There's one," Tito said, one night when he and Manny were driving the streets, not far from the Marine Corps Air Station

Yuma. He had learned that many of the cars they repossessed had been purchased by soldiers who weren't able to keep up with the payments. "That's a beauty," said Tito. "A yellow Camero."

It was dark and raining steadily that night, unusual for southern Arizona. The car was parked in a detached garage with the door left open. Manny checked his list of license plate numbers with his flashlight and confirmed the tag.

"That's one of them," Manny told Tito.

"Let's hook it up, then," said Tito.

Both boys slid into their waterproof ponchos and Manny got out and directed as Tito backed the truck up to the garage. Quickly, they attached the tow bar and chains, lifted the Camero's rear wheels from the ground, and jumped back into the cab of the truck.

As Tito started to drive away, a very large white man with close cropped blond hair jumped out in front of their truck.

"Stop right there, you damn beaners," he screamed.

He was wearing camo pants and no shirt, and he was holding a deer rifle in his right hand and a crowbar in his left. The deer rifle was about waist high, and pointed at Tito.

"Hey, OK man, no problem," Tito said. He stopped the truck and raised his hands. To Manny, he said, "Drunk soldier," out of the side of his mouth.

The big man shot him through the windshield.

Tito slumped in the driver's seat, and Manny jumped from the truck and ran behind it. He kept the vehicle between himself and the big man, who was circling to the passenger side of the truck.

Suddenly, Manny saw a light-haired man walking up the driveway from the street in the pouring rain. He couldn't really tell, but he had the impression that this man was of Indian descent, which wasn't uncommon in Yuma at that time. The man was tall and well proportioned, like a football player on the Mexican National Team. *Eeeh puto,* Manny thought to himself.

Without hesitation, the light-haired man walked up behind the big man, reached around his left side, and took the crowbar out of his hand. The big man turned and received a smart blow from the crowbar across the bridge of his nose. Reaching to protect his face, the big man dropped the rifle, as the light-haired man smashed the crowbar into the side of his knees, first left, then right, and then, as the big man was falling to the ground, he cracked the crowbar down with a two-handed, overhand blow to the man's clavicle breaking the bone by the sound of it. Then he broke the other clavicle. Game over.

Manny rounded the car to the driver's side and opened the door to get Tito out. The light-haired man watched as Manny checked Tito for a pulse; it was still there. The bullet had apparently passed through the soft tissue of Tito's upper arm, but the shattered windshield glass gave Tito small cuts across his face and neck that looked like bad Halloween makeup.

Manny put Tito into a comfortable position on the lawn and went to the light-haired man, who was already on his cell phone with emergency services. "They're on their way," he said to Manny.

"Who are you?" asked Manny.

"Military Police," said the man. "We've been watching PFC

Johnson, sort of keeping an eye out. I saw you back into the driveway, and I figured it might turn ugly."

"Your job is to help people?" asked Manny. "To stand up for people who are in trouble and can't help themselves?"

"Something like that," said the light-haired man. He smiled to himself.

"Wow," said Manny. "I didn't know a job like that existed."

The next day, Manny joined the Marines.

Chapter 24

Clive yawned. He was sitting in a leather chair in the lobby of the Omni Hotel, holding a newspaper, sipping tea in a china cup and glancing at the elevators from time to time. The small teapot sat on the end table next to his chair. He was wearing a Mark 11 aviator's watch made by IWC and designed for astronavigation after World War II. Clive was a horologist, an aficionado of fine British watches. His fine British watch told him that it was nearly ten AM and that he had been sitting in the lobby for three hours.

Across the lobby, Zeke sat at a telephone table, working the daily crossword puzzle in the Atlanta newspaper. They had rented a room in the hotel, so that their presence wouldn't be questioned, and took up their observation points in the lobby. From those spots, they could see the lobby desk, the elevators, the gift shop and the main entry doors. The lobby was busy with tourists and business people, each of whom appeared to have an important place to go.

They had rented the room Saturday late, and spent much of

the evening keeping watch. It was Sunday morning, now, and they had decided that some leisure time in the lobby wouldn't seem out of place to the hotel staff.

So far, neither of them had seen the Accountant. Clive had signaled when he saw a short man exit the elevators, but it turned out to be a false alarm. Zeke looked over at Clive from across the room, and shook his head.

* * *

"Jefe?" said George.

"Si," came the reply.

"I haven't found him yet," said George in Spanish, out of respect.

"I know."

"If I had, he would be dead, of course."

They were speaking on cell phones with mobile call encryption, which assured that the conversation remained private. It was another cost of doing business.

"Of course," said Jefe. He was on the porch of his villa, overlooking the green grass of his oasis, his lawn and the trees that had been brought in and planted in this dusty place. Most of the roads in San Luis del Colorado were dirt roads, or gravel at best. Sandy and dusty and hot. Some paved roads had been installed by the municipality, but they were in rough shape. Except, naturally, for those roads that Jefe had paid for. Those paved roads circled his compound and provided direct access to the airport, to Sonora 40, the major road south, and to Sonora 10 that led into Baja, California.

And that he had provided many good paying jobs to his neighbors in Sonora Rio was not lost on the community. Jefe enjoyed the esteem and recognition of a hometown athlete, people seeing him in the street and stopping to thank him, to pay their respects.

More than once, Jefe had escaped to Baja when the Federales were closing in, and always because he received a timely tip from a well placed source in the police department. And always, that source found himself to be quite a bit richer within a few weeks. At first, he would escape by car, driving his black Mercedes E-class sedan into the desert. Anymore, though, he preferred to travel in his Learjet 75, a vehicle that he was truly proud to own.

With his success, Jefe had upgraded his escape plans, and acquired a home in Grand Cayman, a country that had no extradition agreement with Mexico or with the United States. The Cayman Island government was glad to see wealthy business owners populating their islands, and encouraged property ownership by offering residents no income taxes and private, offshore bank accounts. The island was within easy reach with Jefe's Learjet.

Jefe looked at Carlos, who was standing in the family room, his AR-15 rifle slung across his back. It was a double benefit that Carlos could both fly the LearJet as well as act as Jefe's lieutenant and protector when it was called for. Carlos had been Jefe's friend since elementary school and had always had Jefe's interests at heart. Like the big brother that Jefe never had, Carlos acted as Jefe's protector, confidant and friend from before the time that Antonio Herman Gurrerra was known as Jefe, which was a long, long time ago. Having Carlos close by made Jefe feel much more secure.

"There is one other small problem, Jefe," said George. "One of Mr. Cruz's friends, the man who took the backpack from the coffee shop, was in the lobby of my hotel. I saw him, but fortunately he didn't see me. He spent several hours sitting in the lobby, talking on his phone and reading a newspaper. I think that he might be searching for me."

"Is he a threat?" asked Jefe.

"I don't think so. But he was at the scene of the accident, and then he left with the backpack. I followed him, and he went into an apartment building. When he came out, he was carrying a different backpack. I followed him, and when he left the school library that backpack was empty."

"How do you know it was empty?"

"I took it and examined its contents. Nothing there."

"Are you compromised?" asked Jefe.

"No, just being careful. This man looks competent. And he's been in the wrong place a number of times," said George. "I inquired with the apartment management...apparently his name is Zeke Traynor."

"Will he find you?" asked Jefe.

"No, I've moved out of the hotel."

"You may use one of my houses," Jefe said, "if it will hasten things."

"That is a good thought, Jefe," George said. "Thank you."

"I'll have Carlos arrange it and get you the information, OK?"

"Yes, I can rent a car here," said George, "and get to the house."

"Good," said Jefe.

"Thank you, Jefe. I'll take care of the Cruz thing," George said.

"I know you will," said Jefe, and hung up the phone.

George waited until he heard the click of the distant cell phone breaking the connection. Then he pushed the red button and hung up his phone.

George walked quietly around the perimeter of Centennial Olympic Park, just east of the Omni Hotel that he had left earlier. The air in the park was cool, particularly in the shade.

The trees were beginning to turn color, but the leaves hadn't started to fall yet. They were scrawny trees for a park as large as Centennial Plaza, disproportionally small. George chose a long bench facing east, away from the hotel, beneath a man-made stand of oak trees, and he sat on one end. The concierge was keeping his single travel bag for him, and George would retrieve it later on his way to Jefe's safe house. In the meantime, George stilled himself and thought about Zeke Traynor. He seemed to think and act quickly. He seemed to be a man to respect.

* * *

Manny Lopez was a natural. The Marine Corps had found one of their own, and Manny had found the family that he'd never had. He thrived on the chain of command, the mutual support, the "band of brothers" mentality that permeated every activity.

Manny sailed through boot camp in the Marine Corps Recruit Depot in San Diego, next to the San Diego International Airport, and found his place in the Marine Corps Infantry with two tours in Iraq. During the second tour he won the Navy Cross for dragging two wounded Marines from a bomb site, and then returning to take out a nearby enemy personnel carrier with an M67 hand grenade. Witnesses to the skirmish said that Manny Lopez was relentless, even zealous in his attack.

Later promoted to Gunny Seargent, Manny planned to be a lifer in the Marines until his closest friend in the service died in a training accident. They had called it "friendly fire" and the frustration and the sense of loss took its toll on the young man.

At his next opportunity, Manny left the Marines and moved to Yuma. A month later, a friend told him that the Maricopa County Sheriff's office was hiring Deputies, and Manny drove to Phoenix and applied. With his service record he was hired quickly and went to work.

CHAPTER 25

"4273," she said.

"Hello, Susan," Zeke said. It was Sunday afternoon.

"Hello yourself," said Sally in a breathy voice. "What's the latest?"

"There's been no sign of my friend for a while," said Zeke, "and I haven't had any luck with the other thing, either." He was referring to his efforts to locate George at the Omni.

"Well, you're here, and Eric asked if you'd stay around a few days and help him with another issue that came up."

"Sure," said Zeke.

"Thanks. You've got an appointment this afternoon with someone who's actually going to be there," said Sally, wryly. "Three o'clock at Brown's restaurant. You can walk, it's just east of the Interstate."

"Nice day for it."

"You'll be meeting Mary Anderson. She needs protection from her ex-husband," said Sally.

"OK, what do I need to know?" asked Zeke.

"It's a divorce situation, heading for court next week to divide up the property. The divorce was final several months ago. The ex-husband is ex-army, some Special Forces guy, I'm told, and apparently, he's not happy about the split or about the division of property."

"Got it," said Zeke.

"He's been physical, but only in private. We need to protect young Mary from the possibility of harm until this is finished and she can reposition herself elsewhere."

"Any kids in the picture?"

"Nope," said Sally, "but she's a looker. I just sent a photo of the young lady to your phone. Have fun!"

* * *

At 2:55 PM Zeke was seated in a vinyl booth in the quiet restaurant, with his back to the sidewall of the building. From there, he could see the front door, through the front glass, and the entire dining room, except for the bar and restrooms in the adjoining area. The kitchen was also out of direct view, although he was watching an unexpectedly active server moving in and out of the swinging doors that were fanning warm air and a smell that had to have come from the cooktop.

Zeke had ordered coffee and a slice of apple pie with a thick slice of cheddar on top, and he was enjoying the wait for his three o'clock client. The cheddar softened and had melted perfectly on top of the warm pie, and Zeke admired it as he took another bite.

Mary Anderson entered the restaurant. She glanced at the "Please Wait to be Seated" sign, looked behind her, then looked around and walked directly to Zeke's booth. She sat down heavily, although she didn't appear to be a very heavy girl. Zeke estimated that she was about 5'4" and maybe 120 pounds at most. She had brown hair and wide brown eyes and a very open face. It was a face that reminded him of innocence and trust. It was a pretty face, fine features with clear skin and there was the hint of the smell of lavender lingering, as if it had followed her into the restaurant. It was a face you instinctively didn't want to disappoint.

"Hi, I'm Zeke," he said as he stood to greet her. Nothing was happening outside and no one had followed her, he noted with a glance.

"I know, I'm Mary Anderson," she said. Mary smiled a wide, white smile. She had nice, even teeth. "Good to meet you," she said. They shook hands over the table.

"How can I help…?"

"Oh, call me Mary. It may be nothing, and I don't want to be any trouble, but I may need protection from my ex-husband."

She looked down. "I hope I don't," she said. She looked back at Zeke. "That's what you do, right?"

"We do."

"The court date is next Wednesday," Mary Anderson said. "The judge will be hearing from both sides and dividing up the property." She pouted a little bit.

Her presence had a South American flavor, just a taste Zeke noticed. *She could have been from Rio, or Sao Paulo,* he thought.

"So, my ex-husband isn't happy. It hurts his ego that I left him, and even more so that I won't do what he tells me to do, and be a good little girl, the submissive wife."

"How long have you been divorced," asked Zeke?

"It's been about four months, and it's time to get past this, and move on. But he doesn't want to do that."

"OK, tell me about him."

She reached into her purse and pulled out her phone and showed Zeke a photograph of herself and a young, light haired man on a beach, sipping tropical drinks with an ocean in the background. It was a classic vacation photo, a typical Facebook selfie.

"This was three years ago in Cancun," she said. "He looks pretty much the same today. Short light brown hair, blue eyes, over six feet tall. Steve is very fit, Zeke. He's in the Army and he trains all the time."

"Steve Anderson. He's been physical with you?" Zeke asked.

"Only when we're alone, and only a couple of times, when he was frustrated and angry."

"Did he hurt you badly?" asked Zeke.

"He grabbed me and pushed me this last time. I fell and bruised my side." She rolled her left sleeve cuff up a couple of rolls and showed him a yellow-green bruise outlining four fingers marks and a thumb mark on her forearm.

"Ouch," said Zeke. "OK, we'll make arrangements to keep you safe though the court hearing, and we'll help you get out of the area after that. You'll need to stay with us in a safe house, and you won't be able to call or talk with anyone during that time. I understand there are no children involved?"

"None but my ex-husband," she said and looked at Zeke. He thought he saw her eyes smiling at him a bit.

"You still love him?" asked Zeke.

"He can be charming," said Mary, "but I know that I need to move on."

"Forgive me, but have you been intimate with him since the divorce?"

The blush began to crawl up Mary's neck and reached her ears. She looked away.

"Where are you staying?" asked Zeke.

"I've been staying in our house about ten minutes from here. Why?"

"Your and Steve's house?" Zeke looked at Mary and she nodded. "I suggest that you don't go back there. We'll arrange to get your clothes and personal items for you. What's the address?"

Mary told him. She handed him a key from her key ring.

"I do have one question, Mary Anderson. It's rare that we're hired and the fee is paid in full, in advance. Rather unusual."

"Yes, I would think so," she responded. "And it's not Anderson any longer. I've taken my maiden name back. My name is Cruz, Mary Cruz."

"As in Alberto?"

"My father."

CHAPTER 26

This time Zeke entered his apartment building through the front lobby, and with Mary following him he took the elevator to the third floor. Zeke navigated the hallways while Mary followed alongside him.

"Your father prepaid for your protection," Zeke said, pondering. "So before he left town, he arranged for you to be guarded. Interesting."

"He said that he was concerned for my safety," Mary explained, "but he said that he had to leave to avoid some trouble with his business."

"And you're certain that he left town?" Zeke asked.

"Yes," said Mary. "He called and told me he was on the road. Said we should be able to get back together after this divorce thing is resolved next week."

"Did he tell you where he was heading?" he asked.

"No," Mary said. She looked away.

"So, to keep you safe, we'll start by hiding you in my apartment, while we work out a plan," Zeke said, putting his key in the lock. The "tell" on the door was in place, Zeke noticed; no one had entered while he was away. Still, he had Mary stand around the near corner in the hallway while he checked the apartment. It was clear.

"OK, come on in," Zeke called in a low voice.

Mary stepped around the corner and into Zeke's entry area. She noticed that the apartment was modern and clean, bright and spacious. She passed the kitchen on her left, a bedroom on her right, and entered the open living area ahead of her. Zeke pointed to the sofa and said, "Make yourself comfortable," and Mary stepped around the coffee table and sat down. Zeke locked the door and joined her in the living area.

Zeke checked his cell phone for messages, but there were none.

"Do you have any close family around here?" asked Zeke.

"No, I'm an only child. My mother moved to Miami a few years ago."

"Alberto's ex-wife?" Zeke asked.

"Yes."

"OK, a few rules. You probably already know this, but I need to be sure we're on the same page, OK?"

"OK," said the girl.

"Stay indoors, in the apartment at all times, right?"

"Right."

"Don't tell anyone where you're staying, or even allude to the fact that you're in an apartment. Don't answer your phone, if you can possibly avoid it. If you do answer, don't mention my name or anything about your protection. OK?"

"OK."

"Make up a story in advance about where you are. You went to visit a friend until the court session. Or you're staying in a hotel room because you're afraid. Be ready with the story in advance, before someone asks. If you'd like, I'll work with you on that," Zeke said.

"OK."

"We've got a few places that we use to hide people, and we'll set one of those up and move you tomorrow. In the meantime, Clive and I will take turns staying here with you. Clive Greene owns The Agency, and he's my friend. Totally trustworthy and competent."

"OK."

"You can have the bedroom, Mary," said Zeke. "We'll get your clothing and a toiletries kit from your house. Feel free to use the soap and shampoo in the bath. What kind of food do you like?"

"I'm pretty easy when it comes to food," she said. "No allergies, so just about anything. I don't eat meat, though."

"All right, we'll be Vegan this week. Coffee?"

"Yes, espresso, or very dark roast, if I have a choice. Café Cubano."

"We can do that," said Zeke.

There was a knock at the apartment door.

Zeke looked at the monitor and saw the small woman smiling up at him. "It's Kimmy," he said.

"Hey, Zeke," Kimmy said through the door.

Zeke turned to Mary and mouthed, "Neighbor. She's OK." He opened the door.

"Wine time," said Kimmy. Already moving and not one to allow psychological barriers like a doorway to deter her, Kimmy stepped in past Zeke, down the hall and into the kitchen.

"Oh, I didn't know that you had company," she said as she opened the wine fridge and selected a fresh bottle of Pinot Grigio from inside.

"Hi, I'm Kimmy, from across the hall," she said over her shoulder to Mary. Kimmy turned and busied herself with the corkscrew. "Two glasses or three?" she asked, filling one glass as she spoke.

"Kimmy, this is Mary, a friend of mine. Mary, meet Kimmy. Would you care for a glass of white?" said Zeke.

"Glad to know you, Kimmy," said Mary. "Yes, please."

"Then three," said Zeke. Kimmy poured wine into the other two glasses, and handed them around.

Today, Zeke noticed, Kimmy was dressed in a loose, short sleeve tie-dyed wrap with flat sandals and a white skirt with gold thread trim. The skirt was belted with a wide, purple belt that sported a large gold buckle. As she reached over the coffee table to hand Mary her wine her hair fell away and Zeke noticed her gold earrings, rings decorated with small, colorful feathers.

* * *

During the week before Alberto Cruz was detained by the Secret Service, he had encountered Umberto and Ricardo at El Toro. Following that brief meeting, Cruz knew that the clock had started ticking. What Alberto didn't know was that, after Ricardo reported back to Jefe by phone, George had been dispatched to handle the situation.

As was his habit, George spent most of the first few days in Atlanta gathering first-hand information and in reconnaissance. He checked into his hotel room at the Omni, a very public and busy place- and a first class hotel- and spent the first day on foot. Later, after he felt comfortable with the logistics he rented a car, a Range Rover, and began following Cruz. From Alberto's home, George tracked Cruz, just maintaining a tail, watching for others who might be involved and recording Cruz's patterns. It paid off quickly.

Leaving his south Fulton County home, at one point Alberto Cruz drove to a shopping mall and parked outside a regional chain restaurant. He locked his car and went into the restaurant, where there was a short wait for a table, it being near lunch hour.

George went into the mall, and entered the restaurant at the mall entrance, grabbing a small, two top table in the bar area. The hostess had said, "The bar area is first-come, first-served." That worked for George.

George watched as Cruz unexpectedly stood and hugged a young woman as she approached his booth. She was small and slim, although she was slightly taller than George. She had a dark complexion, maybe South American, and her face was brooding, even angry. Her familiarity with Cruz indicated that she was a close friend or relative. Based on the obvious age difference, it looked like maybe twenty years, George guessed she was a relative.

"May I take your drink order?" A young server interrupted George's thoughts.

"Oh, yes, thank you," said George. "May I have an iced tea?"

"Sweetened or unsweetened," she replied automatically.

"Unsweetened, please."

"Yes, sir, I'll be right back with that."

Obviously distraught, the young woman had reached across the table and had taken Cruz's hands in hers, holding them while she talked rapidly. She looked as if she might be crying. *A niece,* thought George, *or a cousin, perhaps. Or even a daughter.* But there had been no report of Cruz having family in Atlanta.

"Here's your tea, sir," said the server. "Do you know what you'd like to eat?"

"What's that man eating?" asked George, pointing at a nearby table.

The server looked. "That's the fish taco," she said.

"I'll have that, then," he said.

George decided that he would follow the girl and see where she led him.

CHAPTER 27

George was already in his rental car when the young woman left the restaurant. It was a small matter to follow the distraught woman from the mall to her home, and he did so without being noticed. She pulled her red Toyota into the driveway of a one-story brick home, but stopped before she reached the carport. There was a man standing in the driveway, blocking her access.

He was a tall man, and fit, George noted. He had short brown hair and was wearing jeans and a long-sleeved flannel shirt, the sleeves rolled up on his muscular forearms. The man walked to the driver side window and motioned for the young woman to lower her window. She did.

While they spoke, George made a note of the address of the house, and with his small camera took several quick photos of the house and the car she was driving. He noted her license tag. He circled the block, and on his second approach he saw that the woman was out of the vehicle and appeared to be arguing with the man.

The man, obviously angry, started to grab her arms above the elbows, but then thought better of it and looked around for any observers. George was past the driveway and turning the corner at that point.

Interesting, he thought. *They're obviously connected somehow. OK, let's see where this guy leads me.*

* * *

"Is this seat taken?"

Steve turned on his bar stool and saw a short man dressed in blue jeans and a green Polo shirt looking up at him. He seemed very still.

"No, help yourself," said Steve.

The man lifted himself onto the stool with some help from the bar foot rail, and then turned his attention to finding the bartender.

The bar was located in a small retail strip center across and down the street from what used to be Mary and Steve's house. It was a neighborhood place, with dark wooden trim and a polished mahogany bar that looked as if it were a hundred years old. The bar was the centerpiece of the smallish room and the establishment was named Mahogany's. This was clearly a place where people came to drink. Steve had maintained a presence there when he lived in the neighborhood.

The bar area of Mahogany's Bar and Grill was slow at present, awaiting the after work crowd. There was one bar tender serving the small audience of four, three men and one woman.

The third man and the woman were sitting together, chatting idly and sipping colorful drinks. The bar tender made his way down the bar toward Steve.

"Barkeep," said the small man, "may I bother you for a Gin and Tonic? Tanqueray Gin?" The bar tender went to work without saying anything and began mixing the beverage.

"I'm George," said the small man, turning back toward Steve. Steve was drinking his draft beer, looking at the mirror behind the bar. George noticed Steve's forearm tattoo of a military insignia.

"Not much in the mood to talk right now," said Steve, setting his beer on the bar.

"No worries, man," said George. "I'm visiting with my wife, and she decided to go shopping with her sister. I ticked her off this morning, so I have some time to kill, I guess."

Steve said nothing. The bartender approached and set the gin drink in front of George.

George sipped his drink. "Oh, that's good," he said. He took another sip.

"Another beer?" the bartender asked Steve. He nodded.

"You married?" George asked Steve.

"I was," said Steve. "No more of that for me," he said with some bravado.

"Tell me about it," said George. "If I could have a do-over..."

"I know. Can't live with 'em... I'm Steve," he said. "Sorry, I'm just a bit upset at my ex-wife today."

"Just today?" said George. "Because I could live with just one day."

“No, it’s a continuing thing,” said Steve. “Never seems to end.”

George sipped his drink and nodded sagely.

“What did she do this time?” asked George.

“She’s screwing with me in the divorce,” he said. “She’s trying to take all of my property.”

George nodded. “That’s the single reason that I stay married,” he said. “In California, the woman gets everything most of the time.”

“You from California?” asked Steve. “Where abouts?”

“Near L.A.,” said George. “A town called Tarzania. We’ve lived there since I got out of the military.”

“You were in the service?” asked Steve. “What branch?”

“I was in the Air Force,” said George. “Flew C-130’s around the world. You?” George had recognized Steve’s tattoo, but asked the question anyway.

“Yeah, I was in the Army, Special Forces,” said Steve with the blush of pride he always felt about this topic. “Three tours in the Middle East.”

“Impressive,” said George. “Did you see much action?”

“You know,” said Steve, “you prepare and prepare, practice and practice, and then they usually cancel the mission at the last minute. But we had some opportunities to perform.”

“Sure, ‘hurry up and wait,’” said George, to keep the conversation going.

“Yep.”

“So, how did you end up here in Atlanta?” asked George. “Any family here?”

"Not really," said Steve. "My wife has family visiting from Mexico, but nothing permanent. We were stationed at Fort Bragg for my last tour, and after that, Atlanta seemed to have the best job opportunities. My wife is a nurse. Well, my ex."

"Yeah, like I said, we're visiting my wife's sister here. Seems like a nice town."

"It can be," said Steve.

"Your ex-wife has family visiting?"

"Yeah, her father came to Atlanta a couple weeks ago from Mexico. I don't know much about him. I think he's an artist or something," said Steve.

"What's his name?" asked George.

"Why?" said Steve, as he looked at George with his first hint of suspicion.

"I'm a cop," said George. "LA County. I might be able to ask the locals for a favor or something, see what they know about him."

"You think that'd accomplish anything?" said Steve.

"Not sure, but it's possible it might give you some leverage in the property distribution. I mean, is he here legally? Is he wanted for anything or does he have any outstanding warrants? Anything on his record? It might be worth checking out. Where I'm from, that's a routine first step."

Steve thought about it. "Can't hurt, I guess," he said. "You may be right, though," Steve added. "Mary did say that her Dad was being held by the Secret Service about a week ago. They kept him in their offices, I think. And then he left, she said. So, maybe there's something going on there that I could use."

CHAPTER 28

"Are you from around here, Mary?" asked Kimmy, when they were all seated in the living room.

"Mary's actually in town for a couple days," Zeke said. "She's visiting for a job interview, and then she'll be heading home."

"Where's home?" asked Kimmy.

Mary said, "I'm from Arizona."

"From Sedona?" asked Kimmy. "I love Sedona!"

"South of Sedona, actually. Closer to Yuma."

"Oh, down by the border," said Kimmy. "That's pretty country out there."

"Yes, but its time for a move," said Mary. "Where's home for you, Kimmy?"

"I'm originally from Israel," said the small dark-haired woman, "but I've lived in Atlanta for a while."

"How do you like it here?" asked Kimmy.

"Oh, this is a great place to live. There's plenty to do, and people in the south are so friendly, aren't they, Zeke?" she asked.

Yep, they treat you like family, Zeke thought. He nodded.

"So, where are you staying while you're in town, Mary?" asked Kimmy.

"We were working out the arrangements when you arrived," said Mary.

"I wonder if Mary could stay with me while she's here?" Kimmy suggested. "It might be more comfortable for her sharing space with another girl. And she'll be right across the hall. I get a good vibe from you, Mary."

"That's very kind of you," Mary said to Kimmy while looking at Zeke. "Zeke?"

"It might work," he said. "Kimmy's a little bit bohemian, but if you can live with that, it might work."

"I am," said Kimmy, "salt crystals and candles and astrology charts. You can sleep in my second bedroom, I'll clear it out."

"Fine with me," said Mary.

* * *

"Sally told me you called," said Clive. "Said I should meet you here."

They were at the Barnes and Noble store just east of the Interstate, across from the Tech campus. It was 10:00 AM and the noise from the downtown rush hour traffic had subsided. Outside, there was a light misting rain uniformly dampening everything it touched.

Clive was dressed in a summer suit, absent a jacket as he often was, with green linen slacks, loafers and a silk shirt. He wore no socks. His tie was Regimental, and Zeke recognized it as the 4th/7th Royal Dragoon Guards' tie. It was made of silk, with broad red and green alternating stripes. His umbrella matched the tie. Clive was sometimes intentionally ironic with his appointments.

The Royal Dragoon Guards also favored green trousers, thought Zeke.

"Our newest client was a bit of a surprise, I suppose," continued Clive. "I didn't see that coming."

"But from Cruz's point of view, it makes perfect sense. He leaves us protecting his daughter as he makes his escape. Not a bad move, actually." Zeke was wearing jeans and a long-sleeved print shirt and practical tennis shoes. He looked like most of the other customers in the bookstore.

"I guess we need to reassess his abilities, and maybe his role in all of this. He seems to have been somewhat more of a mastermind than we thought," said Clive. "That will bear some review."

"If he's this clever now, it's likely he's been clever all along," said Zeke. "So where is he headed now? Or do you think he's hiding locally?"

"Not sure," said Clive. "I like the odds that he's moving, going somewhere. If he were staying, it seems that he'd be staying close to us."

"Moving on would break all of his habits and eliminate any possible accidental run-in with Jefe's man, the Accountant. It seems most likely that he's heading somewhere else."

"Yes, but where?" asked Clive.

"Cruz speaks Spanish and English. But its Mexican Spanish,

which is different from Castilian Spanish or Cuban Spanish," said Zeke. "He's Hispanic looking. And his contacts are from northern Mexico, but he's running from his contacts. Any one of them in Mexico or here in Atlanta would turn him into Jefe for cash in a hot minute."

"So he'd run north, or south or east," said Clive. "Do you think he took a flight?"

"No, he couldn't carry enough with him on a plane. And he probably has a gun by now. I doubt that he'd want to give that up."

"So bus, car, train…?"

"Cruz likes control. Look at how he set up the Secret Service and sent his neighbor to the exchange at the coffee shop. And he's been agile at avoiding Jefe's people. A train or a bus runs on someone else's schedule, and there's no room to maneuver. Point A to point B, in a prescribed interval. There's a lot of room for him to be discovered, a random sighting or by someone watching the terminals or the security cameras. Could be Jefe's men, or the Secret Service or anyone else with knowledge of his situation. And once he's been discovered, his alternatives are pretty limited."

"So, a car," said Clive.

"That would be my guess," said Zeke. "But not a rental. That would leave a paper trail the Feds would find immediately."

"Even if he used a different identity, a car would give him so much more flexibility. He can stop and go at will; he can divert if he smells trouble; he can delay; or he can abandon the vehicle and find other transport. Sounds right for our Mr. Cruz," Clive added.

"I'd bet that he wanted to get out of here as quickly as possible," said Zeke. "It wouldn't surprise me if he stole a car and jumped on the closest interstate going in his direction."

"That would be Interstate 20 east, or Interstates 75 or 85, north or south," Clive said. "You can access any one of them less than two miles from here."

"Another factor favoring the car theory," Zeke commented.

"So which way?" said Clive.

"To blend in as much as possible, Cruz would go south, to Tampa or Miami…or northeast to New Jersey or New York," said Zeke. They were starting their analysis game again.

"What else is unique about our Mr. Cruz?" asked Clive.

"His daughter. He'll want to be able to monitor that situation, I'm sure," said Zeke. "So, he needs to have eyes and ears on her."

"That would be us, I assume," said Clive.

"Mary mentioned that Cruz had an ex-wife in Miami. That might mean he's heading south."

"If my ex-wife were in Miami, I'd be heading north," said Clive.

* * *

"Where's Mary now? At your apartment?" asked Clive.

"She was, but she met my neighbor Kimmy, and we decided that she'd be more comfortable staying across the hall with Kimmy for the week," said Zeke.

"Well, if she stays put, it would give her an extra layer of protection. No prior connection between Kimmy and her, right?"

"Right. It's fairly random. And the husband shouldn't be able to locate her if he trips across us."

"OK, but we need to stay close and keep her away from the phone," Clive mused. "We should be able to do that."

"Sure. You take the first watch, Clive. Here's Mary's cell phone number. She's expecting you to call her this afternoon. I told her that you'd be keeping an eye on the neighborhood. I'll check on the ex's whereabouts and see if I can catch up with him. I think I might chat with him."

"That could be fun," said Clive. "I'm sorry to miss it."

CHAPTER 29

Alberto Cruz was, in fact, heading south on the Interstate. He was about two and a half hours into his 700-mile journey, driving cautiously, observing the speed limit, using his turn signals and staying in the right hand lanes whenever he could. He was driving a dark blue Toyota Camry, the fifth most stolen car in America. Cruz had stolen the car from a downtown Atlanta surface parking lot, one with an honor system that encourages drivers to find a parking spot and then slip some cash into the right slot in a metal box. It had become too dangerous to stay in Atlanta.

In his trunk was a duffle bag that held his clothing, a blanket, and fifty thousand dollars in large bills pushed into a cardboard banker's box and held shut with packing tape. He'd picked up the money from his house after he'd secured the car and exchanged the license plates with a similar car he found parked in a shopping mall parking garage.

He'd walked into the garage from the mall, aware of the security cameras. Once Cruz found a duplicate vehicle, he opened the trunk as if putting his bag in, blocking the camera while pretending to be looking for something. Within 90 seconds, the license tags had been exchanged, and he closed the trunk and walked back into the mall. At the mall door, Cruz slipped off his latex gloves and tossed them, with the screwdriver, into a trash bin. He'd slid the license plate under his belt, on his back, beneath his shirt.

Cruz wandered around the stores for a half hour, then exited the mall on the other side. The new tags went on his car a few moments later in a surface parking area. He had backed in with his rear bumper facing the concrete half wall behind the car, which gave him cover. Then he got into the car and drove to the Interstate. *Drive like an old woman,* he thought to himself.

There was an H&K VP9 handgun in his front waistband. It fired a 9-millimeter bullet and held 15 rounds in the magazine. It was a very highly rated weapon, and Cruz had practiced with one like it many, many times. This one had been purchased for cash from a dealer at the Atlanta Gun and Knife Show earlier this month. No background check and no questions asked.

Cruz was wearing a white Guayabera shirt over a textured wife-beater tee shirt and a pair of beige slacks. In the passenger seat, sitting next to Cruz, was Alejandro Chile, his nephew, his sister's boy. Alejandro was in his early twenties and was wearing a loud print tourist shirt, untucked with the top three buttons unbuttoned, and a pair of cargo shorts. Both men had open toed sandals on their feet, and neither wore socks. Alejandro wore a large gold chain around his neck. They were silent until they saw the exit sign for Tifton, Georgia.

"Can we stop for the night?" Alejandro asked.

"No, but we can stop and eat, if you'd like," said Cruz, looking at his watch and the clock on the dashboard, calibrating and calculating.

"There are thousands of hotel rooms there, according to that sign," said Alejandro. "Seems like a safe place to stay." He was already bored, tired of riding.

"This is a nine-hour trip," said Cruz. "We should get into it before we stop anywhere."

Alejandro turned and looked out the passenger side window. To Cruz, it felt as if his nephew were pouting.

"You like baseball, right?" Cruz asked.

"Yes, I sure do," said Alejandro.

"Well, we'll be staying right down the street from the Marlin's baseball field," Cruz continued. "You'll be able to walk to the stadium."

"They're not playing now, are they?"

"Sure, they play into early October this year," answered Cruz. "They play 162 games. And then there's the play-offs."

"So we can catch a Marlin's game?" Alejandro seemed engaged again.

"Maybe more than one," said Cruz.

Cruz glanced right. The boy was smiling again.

Chapter 30

Zeke watched as the man approached Mary Cruz's house from the rear, stepping over the low fence and staying close to the hedge in the twilight. He was almost silent as he reached the back porch.

As quietly as possible, he stepped up on the porch and listened. Inside the house the television was playing. Lights were on in the kitchen and the family room. The man looked through the kitchen window and into the family room with its flat screen television against the far wall, and the sofa facing it, its back to the kitchen. The kitchen was the first room the man would enter through the back door, followed by the dining room that opened into the family room. *Maybe five steps, maybe fifteen feet. Maybe three quiet seconds,* thought Zeke.

There was no one else in the house. Zeke had arrived several hours ago and had staged the house. Then he found a spot to wait in the bathroom with the small window over the tub. The window overlooked the back yard. He watched for a minute.

The man on the porch hadn't knocked or rung the bell. He

hadn't made any noise, a fact that Zeke took as a sign of the man's competence and training.

He figured that Steve Anderson would return to talk with his wife. In fact, he'd had Mary call Steve and scream at him, saying she was still angry and that she was throwing out some of his things, in order to flush him out and save some time. Zeke thought that confrontation would be necessary and, he thought, there's no time like the present.

Zeke stepped quietly to the bathroom door, and then to the short hallway that led to the family room. Nothing was happening yet. Then, in a moment, the man walked past Zeke, watching the couch and watching the room. He entered the room competently. Both of his hands were empty, Zeke noticed, and there was no sign of a weapon, nothing stuffed inside his belt.

The man, Steve Anderson, Zeke could tell from the picture now, approached the couch and looked around in surprise. There was no one else in the family room, or in the house, actually.

"Hello, Steve," said Zeke from the hallway.

Steve Anderson spun to his right, which, if he were carrying a weapon would have been the most efficient movement. He actually raised his right hand to his waist before he realized it was empty. *He's a tall man, maybe six foot three,* Zeke thought. *And he looks fit.*

"Who are you?" asked Steve. He took a step back, increasing the space between himself and Zeke. "Where's Mary?"

"She's not here, Steve. She's somewhere safe."

"Hey, she called and said that she was going to throw out

my stuff." Steve's attitude was replacing the surprise he'd felt. "Where is she?"

Zeke changed the subject. "You didn't knock," he said.

"It's my house, man," said Steve. "I don't have to knock."

"Actually, that's up in the air until next week, isn't it?" asked Zeke. "Right now, as I recall, there's a restraining order for you to stay away."

"Watch your mouth," said Steve. "This is my business and my wife's business. There's no room for you in it."

"Your ex-wife, right?" Zeke pushed another of the man's buttons. Steve's face was getting tight like a clenched fist.

"You bastard, this doesn't involve you. Who are you, anyway?"

"Just a close friend of Mary's." Zeke pushed a little harder.

"That bitch."

"You can't blame her because her father set it up." *Which is true in a way*, thought Zeke.

"When? Before he left for Miami?" Steve was puzzled for a moment. "He set you up with her?"

"Yep, before he left for Miami," Zeke repeated.

"Mary said he was going back to the Orange Bowl neighborhood," Steve said. "Where her mother lives. Said it was a place where her Dad knew people." He thought for a moment, and then looked at Zeke. "Mary never mentioned you."

"Probably trying to prevent being treated like a punching bag…again," said Zeke.

"I'll kill you." Steve's rising anger telegraphed his intention as he stepped across the small space toward Zeke. Right foot, left, and then right again as Steve threw a straight punch aimed at Zeke's face.

Zeke stepped into the punch with his left foot, and easily diverted the fist with his forearm. The punch ended up over Zeke's left shoulder, and Zeke grabbed and held Steve's shirt-sleeve with his left hand as he twisted to the right. He moved, and both of Steve's legs were swept aside.

In a continuous motion, and with a twist of Zeke's upper body, Steve was suddenly lying face up, flat on the hardwood floor, his legs against the wall pointing toward the ceiling. Zeke kept his handgrip on Steve's right forearm, and kneeling into the man, he used a wristlock to hold him down while giving him two sharp, straight jabs to the solar plexus and one to the throat. Steve began gasping for air and rolling around on the floor. The action had lasted less than four seconds.

"Sweeping Loin Throw," Zeke said to himself. "Simple but elegant." Zeke considered Judo a complete art. It teaches you what to do both before and after the takedown. As always, Zeke felt calm, centered and balanced, both physically and mentally.

He smiled and walked out the back door.

CHAPTER 31

Having finally caught his breath, Steve sat against the wall in the house and probed various tender spots on his back, stomach, sides and neck. He remembered taking a swing at the guy who said he was Mary's boyfriend, and then he was on his back, fighting to breathe. After a while, he slowly got to his feet and fought off a round of nausea and short breath before things started to stabilize again.

Hunched over and holding himself together with both hands, Steve stumbled out the back door of the house and across the yard. He stepped over the low fence gingerly, looked both ways and started down the street. He walked a short ways and turned in to Mahogany's.

Although it wasn't very late, there were only a handful of people in Mahogany's. Two guys were at the far end of the bar, watching what sounded like golf on television. Couples drinking and talking occupied three of the six small booths. There was one single woman at the near end of the bar. Steve went to the bar and gingerly lifted himself onto a seat two stools away from anyone else.

"Hey, Steve," said the bartender. "Draft?"

"Not tonight, Howie," said Steve. "Seven and seven."

Howie shot Steve with his finger and turned to mix the drink.

* * *

"I thought I might find you here," said George as he pulled himself up on the barstool next to Steve. "Mind if I join you?"

"No, sure," said Steve. He was working on his third seven and seven. At least the pain in his chest and back had subsided.

George waved at Howie, who had one eye on a replay of last weekend's PGA golf tournament, and ordered a draft beer. Howie pulled the beer.

"You know," George said, just to be saying something, "the old English word draught actually means 'to pull'". George was watching Howie fill the glass down near the television set. Howie returned, set a cardboard coaster in front of George, lightly salted the coaster to keep it from sticking to the glass and placed the glass in the center of the coaster. He nodded at George and moved down the bar. Steve sipped on his drink.

"So, how're things going?" asked George. "Any change in your relationship?"

"Nope," said Steve. "No change. I'm still living in my rented room at my buddy's place and we're still heading for court next week to divide up the property."

"That sucks," said George.

"Sure does," said Steve, and he seemed to ponder the point

for a moment.

"I checked on Alberto Cruz, the father-in-law you mentioned," said George. "Talked to a guy on the Atlanta PD. Professional courtesy and all that."

"Anything there?" asked Steve with some interest.

"Might be," said the small man. "I spoke with a Sergeant Day at Atlanta police headquarters. They think he may be in the country illegally. Of course, that would be an INS matter, but the INS often informs the local police about people they know of but haven't gotten to yet."

"So the Detective you spoke with has information that Cruz is an illegal alien?"

"That he doesn't have a work visa or a green card is more like it. He can only stay in the country a short time. They expect that he'll go back or be deported at some point," George lied. "You might be able to make some trouble for your ex- if you can keep tabs on Alberto Cruz. Just let me know what you find out, and I'll be glad to share it with the police."

"Sure, thanks," said Steve, with some interest.

* * *

"I called Tracy Johnson on my way here, Zeke. Gave her the Miami information about Cruz," said Clive. "She sounded grateful and asked how I got the lead."

"Did you tell her?" asked Zeke.

"I did. I told her that Cruz had mentioned an ex-wife in Miami at one point, and that we'd followed up on that information."

"Did you mention Steve Anderson?" asked Zeke.

"Didn't see a need to," said Clive. "Seems like that might lead to problems for our new client, too."

"Yes, and the result will be the same, I'm sure."

"Seems like it," said Clive. They were sitting at a table in the Atlanta Breakfast Club, a short order place, sipping coffee. Their order was on the grill.

Zeke sat at an angle, where he could see both the front door and the kitchen door, which, he knew, led to the back entrance of the restaurant. It was a small, rectangular building with the only doors on the front and the backside. The front door looked across a small parking lot to Ivan Allen Jr. Blvd. Across the street were Pemberton Place and the Georgia Aquarium.

There were a handful of tables occupied this morning. The patrons were a mix of students and tourists and downtown business people and one cable repairman, judging by the label on his blue work shirt.

"Did Miss Johnson share her plans, now that she has that information?" asked Zeke.

"No. But I think it's clear that they have to go and get Cruz and bring him back, at least as a person of interest. The Secret Service has a lot invested in Alberto."

"They do indeed," said Zeke. "It'll be good to see him again."

* * *

Tracy Johnson was, at last, in a much better mood. With the tip she'd received from Clive Greene, they should have no trouble finding Cruz in Miami, and when they found him he would be returned to Atlanta, she thought. She knew that Zeke was behind the fact that she was given Cruz's whereabouts, not Fitch. They had spent some time together, and they both seemed to be enjoying it.

Tracy was on hold with the Miami field office of the Secret Service, waiting for the Special Agent to pick up the phone. She put her hand over the mouthpiece and twisted toward Ron.

"Ron, tell Fitch that we'll need travel vouchers to Miami. We probably need to leave tomorrow morning," she said.

"Already in the works, Tracy. I'm way ahead of you, as always." Ron smiled.

"Hawthorne," said a voice on the other end of Tracy's line. She waved in Ron's direction and twisted back to her desk.

"Yes, sir," said Tracy. She introduced herself and provided her identification information. "We have a reliable lead that puts a person of interest in a counterfeiting and homicide case here in Atlanta on the road to Miami," she continued.

"Literally on the road?" asked Hawthorne.

"Yes, sir. We're told that he's heading to a neighborhood he's familiar with, the area around the Orange Bowl," said Tracy.

"Marlins Park," said Hawthorne, "baseball. About 7th Street and 17th, northwest. They tore the Orange Bowl down a few years back, 2008 or 2009."

"OK, well, that neighborhood. Apparently he spent some time there at some point in the past. We lost him after an exchange went bad. He's driving and should probably arrive sometime late today or tomorrow morning."

"You're in it because of the counterfeiting?" asked Hawthorne.

"Yep," said Tracy.

"So he's probably not armed and dangerous?"

"Doubtful, but be careful anyway," said Tracy.

"OK, e-mail the details and a picture, and we'll watch for him. We should be able to pick him up, no problem," said Hawthorne. He gave Tracy his e-mail address. "Want us to hold him here for you?"

"Sure, we'll be down tomorrow. We're arranging the flights now."

"Need us to pick you up?" asked Hawthorne.

"That would be great. I'll e-mail our flight information, too," said Tracy.

"At your service," said Hawthorne with a smile.

CHAPTER 32

Overall, George was not displeased with the progress of his search. He had taken time out for preparation, which had slowed his active search for Cruz, but it would pay off in the long run. He was pretty sure that Steve would turn into a good source of information about Cruz, also.

One of Jefe's Atlanta houses had been provided for him, and George had spent quite a bit of time getting it ready for the visitors he anticipated hosting in the very near future. The house was a one-story ranch in the northern suburbs of Atlanta. It had three bedrooms and three baths, and a double garage. George had spent two full days modifying one of the smaller bedrooms and the garage.

First, he spent several hours measuring and sizing the windows, doors and hardware in the bedroom. He removed closet doors, grills and grates, light fixtures, a mirror, convenience outlets, switches and hinges. In addition to the Range Rover he'd rented downtown, George arranged for a panel van that he used while working on the house. He used it to make a run to the local home improvement warehouse. There he purchased power tools and a variety of bolts, screws, hooks, locks and hardware to replace what he had removed and to enhance the security of the room.

* * *

It was a hot ninety degrees when Tracy and Ron stepped out of the Miami Airport terminal building, and into a waiting Crown Vic. The air outside smelled like stagnant diesel fumes, trapped under the airport's "departures" overpass. A younger Secret Service agent, a Hispanic woman who introduced herself as Carmen, had met Tracy and Ron as they deplaned. She was wearing casual slacks, a tank top and dress shoes with four-inch heels.

The car was in a "No Parking" zone at the curb near the baggage claim. They put their carry-on luggage in the trunk, and Carmen slid into the driver's seat. Tracy sat next to her, and Ron got into the back seat.

"The badge is good for something," she said as she lifted the sun visor above her head. Tracy read the sign on the opposite side, "Official Government Business," upside down.

"We appreciate the lift to headquarters," said Ron. He caught her eye and smiled to Carmen in the rearview mirror.

"Have you been to Miami before?" Carmen asked.

"No," said Tracy, while simultaneously, Ron said, "Not for a long time."

"Do you know if they've detained Cruz yet?" asked Tracy.

"Yes, he was picked up this morning near the ballpark. A team of agents spotted his car when he arrived, Georgia tags, and called in for backup. They found him sleeping in a furnished apartment and took him without incident. They got him while you were on the flight down."

"Can we see him?"

"That's where we're heading now," said Carmen.

* * *

Secret Service headquarters in Miami was located in distinct buildings about 10 miles west of the airport. The buildings – there were two of them on the campus – looked more like two passing cruise ships than office buildings. On their sides, the buildings' metal skin looked like giant cheese graters reflecting in the south Florida sun. *Some form of Art in Public Places,* thought Tracy, *and the buildings were the art, supposedly.* They entered the driveway.

Carmen pointed the car toward the far building and turned into an entry road marked "Secret Service – private." They approached a guardhouse and Carmen lowered her window and flashed her badge. The guard stepped out into the humid heat, and made a note on his clipboard.

"May I see your identification, please?" he asked Tracy. She handed it across Carmen to the guy, and he looked at Ron expectantly. Ron passed his up front.

The guard was a tall, thin, angular man, with hollow cheeks that gave him a specter-like appearance. He was in a brown long-sleeved shirt and wore a brown belt around his waist and across his chest. He had sweat stains visible in several places on his shirt. There was no breeze at all.

In a moment, the identification and badges were handed back to Tracy and Ron, and Carmen rolled the window up quickly, to cool the passenger compartment. The guard hit a switch and the barrier was lifted, and Carmen drove through and into the parking lot, where she circled twice looking for a shady parking spot.

* * *

"This is Steve," said the voice on the phone.

"George here, Steve, thought I'd check in. Have you heard any more about where Alberto Cruz is?" George was making the rounds, calling his contacts again to see what new information had come to light.

"I have, actually," said Steve. "My wife called. She was crying because the Feds arrested her father again, in Miami. From what I could understand, they brought him back here to Atlanta."

"I see," said George. "Does she want your help now?"

"I think so," said Steve. "It's hard to tell what she wants, though. I guess it depends on what day it is."

"When we last spoke, you said she was in hiding," said George. *Hiding from you,* he thought.

"Yes. But she told me where she is. She wants to get together and talk, and see if I can help her with her father. Apparently, he's looking at some serious jail time."

"Well, you said he was running from the FBI or something. That sounds pretty serious to me, Steve," said George.

"No, the Secret Service. It is serious, I think."

"So, where is she hiding? A shelter?"

"No," laughed Steve. "She's just staying with a girlfriend. Sounds like a sleepover or something."

"No police?" asked George. "It seems like there'd be some police guard or something. I don't want you to get in trouble if you go there, my friend."

"She said no. She said there's some guy her Dad hired to protect her, but he's not around. She's actually not far from the Georgia Tech campus," said Steve, "in Midtown. There's a new apartment complex there."

"I'm heading for Midtown later today," said George, quickly. "Why don't I go by while I'm there and make sure there's no guard or anything, before you show up.

"Would you, man? That would be great."

"Sure, no problem."

Steve gave George the address and apartment number.

"I'll call her and tell her I need to stop by this afternoon for a minute," said Steve. "One thing confuses me, though."

"What's that?"

"Well, remember, I told you about the guy who sucker punched me at my old house?"

"Sure, the new boyfriend," George said.

"I asked Mary about that. Well, I yelled at her about it, actually."

"And?" said George.

"And she acted like she had no idea what I was talking about."

CHAPTER 33

"Welcome back, Mr. Cruz," said Fitch. They were locked in an interrogation room borrowed from the Atlanta police at police headquarters in Midtown. Fitch, Tracy and Ron were sitting on one side of the table, and Cruz, in an orange prison jumpsuit was sitting on the other side of the table. He was handcuffed to a D-ring that was welded to the metal table in front of him. The table was welded to the floor.

Cruz looked at Fitch.

"You disappeared," stated Fitch. "We had a deal, and you skipped out."

Cruz thought for a moment. "Surely you can't blame me," said Cruz. "You saw what happened to the poor man who took my place."

"Did you know that would happen?" asked Tracy.

"I feared that it might," said Cruz. "This is why I came to you in the beginning."

"But you had no prior knowledge of this incident?" asked Fitch.

"I did not," Cruz responded.

Cruz's English seems to have improved pretty dramatically, Tracy thought to herself.

* * *

Mary answered her cell phone. "Hello?"

"Mary, this is Zeke. Just a question."

"OK, sure," she said.

"When your Dad left town, did you know where he was heading?"

There was silence on the line.

"Mary?" said Zeke.

"He told me not to tell anyone," she said.

"But you told Steve, right?" said Zeke.

"I didn't mean to, though. We were arguing about Dad, and it just came out. Like, Steve was asking if I was hiding behind my father, accusing me, and I just said that he's not around, he's on his way back to the old neighborhood in Miami. Something like that," she said.

* * *

"So you have found him," Jefe replied to George's news. They were speaking on the secured phones, the ones with mobile call encryption, two thousand miles apart.

"Si, Jefe," said George, in Spanish. "He was in Miami. He was returned to Atlanta by the Secret Service. He's in custody for trying to flee. This will make things simpler."

"You mean your informant," said Jefe.

"Yes, I'll know the logistics of his whereabouts. It will only be a matter of time," he said.

"You'll make an example of him?" asked Jefe.

"I will," said George.

"Good."

* * *

George, the Accountant, was dressed in a hoodie with the Tech school colors, an old gold background with "Yellow Jackets" lettered across the front in black. His small stature gave him the appearance of a student. The hood was up as he entered the apartment lobby, and he looked away from the security camera as he passed by.

George walked to the stairwell and up three flights of stairs. He turned to the right and found apartment 315. He paused a moment, listening, and then knocked on the door.

Chapter 34

They were annoyed with each other. Mary had talked on the phone, and then told Kimmy that Steve was coming by to talk with her. Kimmy said, "No way."

"Kimmy, you don't understand. I love this guy. He's changed, I've seen him change," she added, speaking quickly, trying to convince Kimmy. "He's not the same guy who I divorced. He's a different man, I'm sure of it. He said he loves me. He even said that he doesn't care about the property. He just wants me back. Besides, I'm tired of just sitting around this apartment."

"Look, Mary, Zeke said that we're supposed to stay out of contact with anyone until next week," Kimmy reminded her. "I should have taken your cell phone away."

"I'm so stressed." Mary pouted and went out on the balcony and lit another cigarette.

Kimmy had just started washing the dishes when she heard the knock. Mary was sitting in a chair on the small balcony, smoking the cigarette and staring out into the street. Looking anywhere except at Kimmy.

Kimmy said, "I'll get it," and shut off the water. She wiped her hands as she walked to the door, expecting Zeke with a load of groceries. Or possibly Steve, who she would tell to leave.

"Who's there," she called out, as she unlocked the door.

"Just me," said a muffled voice as Kimmy turned the knob. Then she hesitated, not recognizing the voice, but it was too late. The door opened in on her and knocked her into the wall behind it. Then she was looking at the barrel of a .357 Chief's Special. It was a handsome gun, with a matte black finish instead of the usual stainless steel.

This was a smaller gun, but it fit the hand of the small man carrying it perfectly. In his comfortable grip, it looked much larger than it actually was.

Kimmy said, "Oh, shit," and then, "Wait, you're not Steve..." as she started to piece together the situation.

"No, I'm not. I'm George," he said.

* * *

"4273," she said.

"Hello, Toni," Zeke said. *Hello Sally, he thought.* It was Thursday, about noon.

"No messages," she continued.

"Have you gotten the information we requested?" Zeke asked Sally.

"Almost done," said Sally. "Will call you when it's ready."

* * *

"I was trying to avoid being killed," said Cruz. "The small man will kill me. He is here because Jefe sent him."

"Mr. Cruz, I don't think you've been giving us the whole story," said Fitch. "You seem to be picking and choosing what you share with us. We don't like to be lied to."

"You didn't mention that you were supplying a substitute at the coffee shop." Fitch ticked his left little finger with his right index finger, counting offenses. "You didn't tell us that your daughter was in town." Tick.

"I couldn't, I had to protect my daughter. That's why I came here to Atlanta in the first place," said Cruz.

"You told us that you were fleeing from Jefe," said Fitch. "Another lie," tick.

"No, no, that is very true," said Cruz.

Fitch looked at the camera, recording Cruz's interview. He looked at Ron and at Tracy, sitting across from Cruz. Then he took out a fresh pad of paper and a pen.

"Alright, Mr. Cruz, let's start at the beginning again."

Fitch continued to question Cruz about his involvement with Jefe, while Cruz acted obtuse.

"Perhaps we should let him go, Tracy," said Fitch. "Release him on his own recognizance."

Ron smiled and thought to himself, *Checkmate.*

"Perhaps we should discuss that," said Cruz. "I believe that I have information about Jefe that you might find very valuable. I know specific things that I observed when in his employ."

"Like what?" said Fitch.

"Deliveries…you know, names and addresses of shipments." Cruz was watching Fitch's eyes for reaction. "And more names… middle men, even his advisors and friends."

"More than the names you've given us?" asked Ron.

"Yes, more. But, of course, I want immunity. And protection. Good protection, better than the Marshalls. Jefe does not fool around with amateurs. They are sending professionals after me."

"You lost your immunity when you ran," said Tracy. "You have to start over again."

"I have more to share," said Cruz.

"Tell us what you have, and I'll talk with the federal prosecutor, and see what we can arrange," said Fitch. "She'll want to interview you."

"Very well," said Cruz.

"But for now, you'll be staying with us, courtesy of the federal government."

"I expected no less," said Alberto Cruz.

* * *

"There is another option, Boss," said Tracy as they took a break from questioning Alberto Cruz.

Fitch was getting tired. "What's that, Tracy?"

"Your friend, Clive Greene. If Cruz hired him for protection, and we know that he's being hunted by Jefe's man, why don't we release Cruz into Clive's custody and use him to flush out the counterfeiters?"

"Yes, good, like bait," said Fitch. "We should be able to use him to get to this killer, and from there to Jefe's organization. We may be able to stop a major counterfeiting operation. Or at least expose it. I'll call Clive."

* * *

"It was smart to have Cruz released into your custody," Zeke said to Clive.

"Seemed like the right thing to do," answered Clive. "Mr. Fitch seemed almost anxious for us to step in."

"Anxious enough that he lent you the printer plates and some of the counterfeit money?" asked Zeke. "Impressive."

"Yes, well, apparently this counterfeiting operation is very important to the Secret Service. Or at least to the Atlanta Secret Service."

"Now all we need is contact with the killer."

Chapter 35

Kimmy and Mary were riding in the back of the rented panel van. It was a white panel van with no rear windows, and with a "BellSouth" logo and advertisement on both sides. The exterior looked like a utility van, and the driver, George, was dressed in coveralls with a matching BellSouth logo over the left side of his chest. He had a hard hat on the seat next to him, along with a tool belt that resembled that of a telephone repairman.

The rear of the vehicle had been cleaned out, leaving only a bench seat and some empty, built-in cabinets. The only door, the rear door, was locked from the outside.

Kimmy and Mary were handcuffed in the back of the van, hands behind their backs, and a third pair of cuffs connecting the two others. Because of this, they were forced to sit at an awkward angle, making their balance on the narrow seat precarious. They each had a half dishtowel in their mouth, secured there by a couple rounds of duct tape circling each of their lower faces. Only Kimmy wore shoes.

After entering the apartment, George had tased Kimmy and

cuffed her, and then taken Mary by surprise. He showed her the gun, stuffed a dishrag in her mouth, and dragged her back into the living room. George handed her the handcuffs. With the gun at her neck, George standing behind her behind the sofa, she had put her hands in the cuffs, one by one, and tightened them. He then took the towel and, using a large knife from his pocket, he slit the dishtowel in two, and stuffed half into Kimmy's mouth. Then he wrapped duct tape around her head, twice, to keep it there.

"Now let's make a phone call," George said to Mary.

He pulled Mary down off the couch onto the living room carpet, and twisted her, face down. He kneeled on her back, his knees just below her shoulder blades, and with the gun in his right hand he grabbed a handful of her brown hair and pulled her head up.

"Your father's phone number, please, Mary," George demanded.

She recited it for him. George gave Mary specific instructions, then took her cell phone and dialed.

"Hola," said Cruz, as he answered his cell phone. He could see by the Caller ID that it was his daughter, Mary, calling.

"Papa," she said. She sounded frightened and out of breath.

"Si, what's wrong?" Cruz's immediately thoughts went to the divorce and that man, Steve, who had hurt her in the past.

"Papa, this man says you must trade with him," continued Mary. "He's hurting me. He says he'll kill me if you don't bring him your plates and the money. Papa, what are these "plates" he's talking about?"

"Don't worry, Mary," said Cruz. "I'll give it all to him. What does this man look like?"

"No need for silly questions, Cruz," said George. "What I look like is not important. Get the money and the plates together, and I'll call you later with instructions. You have two hours before I call again."

"OK," said Cruz.

"And, no Federales, no police."

"OK," said Cruz. The phone went dead in his hand.

"That was unexpected," Clive said to Zeke, conversationally. He was sitting in the desk chair in a King Suite room at the Residence Inn hotel, Midtown. Zeke and Cruz were sitting on the couch. The coffee table, with three empty paper coffee cups was between them. The television was on but muted, replaying a soccer game.

Zeke looked at his watch. It was three minutes after 2:00 PM.

* * *

George had loaded both women onto the freight elevator, which he stalled on the third floor using a small brick, and he had taken them directly down to the garage and into the back of the van. He'd noticed earlier that the maintenance staff went to lunch every day at one o'clock, and that no one else used the freight elevator unless they were moving in or out. No one was moving today.

"Don't make any noise," he warned them both, "or I'll slit your throat." He pointed his knife at Kimmy.

She nodded, and he closed and locked the panel van's back door. In a moment, the engine started and the van moved forward.

The white utility van drove along, stopping and starting in city traffic, accelerating onto an on-ramp, and picking up speed until it was headed out of the city. It felt like a freeway ride, smooth with some occasional deceleration and acceleration, probably when passing other cars. They drove for what seemed like a half hour before they stopped and the engine went silent.

A few moments later, the rear door to the panel van opened. They were inside a double garage, with the garage door closed. George unlocked the third pair of handcuffs, and, Taser in hand, took Mary out of the van. He relocked the cuffs to Kimmy and to a D-ring on the wall, and locked the van door and walked Mary into the house through the connecting door. There was a short, windowless utility area off the garage with a washer and dryer in it, and then the kitchen. The kitchen was a galley-style area that flowed through into a small dining room. She saw two straight-backed chairs in the dining room, and that was all.

George sat Mary in one of the chairs, attached her handcuffed wrists to the chair, and went back to the garage to get Kimmy. Mary was crying.

* * *

The bedroom that the women found themselves in was a small, 8'x 10' room with an 8' ceiling, a closet without a closet door and a window. The window, which faced the small, fenced back yard had been covered over with two sheets of ¾ inch plywood. These were bolted with recessed Allen bolts firmly to four 2'x 6' studs which had taken the place of the original interior window trim. These studs had been bolted to the wall studs that surrounded the window inside the dry wall.

The interior door, previously a builder's grade hollow core wooden door, had been replaced with a solid metal door in a metal frame, which was also firmly affixed to the wall studs surrounding the door. There was a double-key deadbolt on the door, a lock that could be opened with a key from either side. The door closed tightly as a smooth unit and was almost soundproof. The ceiling light fixture had been removed, as had the carpeting, closet doors, and all hardware.

The light switch and convenience outlets had been disconnected at the fuse box and sealed off; they were no longer functional. Blank plates covered their former locations. The air conditioning duct, a 4" x 8" opening in the floor had been covered with a wire grid, bolted to the exposed subfloor. The effect was a dark, quiet room that offered no hope of escape.

In the floor, near each of the four corners of the room, George had affixed a large ring, also bolted to the floor joists supporting the plywood subfloor. He had just finished connecting Mary and Kimmy, each to a ring in an opposite corner, by threading their respective handcuffs through the rings. The women were presently sitting on the floor, their feet about 4 feet from each other, legs splayed, gagged and hands behind them, cuffed to the floor.

"I trust that you'll be comfortable here," said George to the gagged women. “I don’t expect to be gone very long.”

With that, he left and they heard the solid sound of the lock turning in the metal door.

George drove the panel van to a nearby parking lot, parked it and switched vehicles. He was in the Range Rover again. It was a much better ride.

CHAPTER 36

"Mr. Cruz," said the voice on the phone. It was the same voice that had called before, the man who had Mary.

"Si," said Cruz.

"You have what I want?" asked George.

"Si, the money and the plates," said Cruz. Zeke nodded encouragingly as he spoke.

"Go to the Centennial Plaza in twenty minutes and walk toward the Peachtree Plaza hotel, the round building. Stop when you get to Olympic Park Drive, and I'll be watching. I'll call you and pick you up from somewhere near there in a tan Range Rover. Come alone. If you're followed, or anyone is with you, you won't see me or your daughter again," said George.

"I understand," said Cruz. "I'll be there. Just don't hurt her."

* * *

Kimmy and Mary sat facing each other, shackled to the floor. Kimmy said, "We don't have a lot of time. I'd guess about an hour or so, before he comes back."

Mary looked at Kimmy. She was still in shock from the abduction.

"Took him about 30 minutes to get us here from my place, right?"

Mary nodded. *How did Kimmy get free of the gag?* she wondered.

"So, assuming that he's really after your Dad, he'll have to go back and pick him up. Now that he has you to bargain with, I mean." Kimmy looked at Mary quizzically.

"Oh, you're wondering about the gag? Mine was a bit loose, so I brushed it off on this nail in the wall here," said Kimmy.

Mary looked at the wall and then nodded. It was dark, but she didn't see the nail.

"So, first thing, we need to get out of here," said Kimmy. Mary nodded again, not certain how to do that.

"Here, I'll help you," said Kimmy, standing up. Her handcuffs were still on the floor, attached to the D-ring, but lying open. Kimmy smiled.

"Now, Mary," Kimmy said as she crossed the small room, "we need to be really quiet, right?"

Mary nodded. As Kimmy leaned down, her skirt rose slightly and Mary saw a small Star of David tattoo on her right thigh, above the hemline.

Kimmy reached behind Mary's head and loosened the duct tape. The tape relaxed, and Mary was able to spit out the small towel.

"How did you do that?" Mary asked.

"Mine were just loose," Kimmy said again. "I guess he didn't tighten them enough when he put them back on me. Let me see your hands."

She leaned forward and a moment later, Mary felt the handcuffs release, and then heard them fall to the floor. She stood up slowly, still stiff from the ride in the van.

Kimmy had her back turned to Mary and was standing on one leg, pulling her shoe back on.

* * *

Fifteen minutes later, Cruz was in Atlanta's Centennial Park, at the corner of Andrew Young International Boulevard and Olympic Park Drive. It was Thursday, just after six o'clock in the evening, and attendance in the park was sparse. There were no concerts or events scheduled for this late September evening.

George had made the phone call from his parked car, just down the street from the meeting place. He watched as Cruz appeared with a large, blue duffel bag in his hand, looking anxiously for the Accountant.

George put the Range Rover in gear and rolled slowly toward Cruz. The Range Rover, currently a popular vehicle with the yuppie crowd, was a light tan with brown accents and had dark tinted windows. It was just what an Atlanta soccer Mom might use to deliver her children to school in the morning.

As the SUV approached Cruz, he stepped to the curb. George hit the switch and dropped the window halfway, and Cruz looked inside.

"Throw the bag in the back seat, Mr. Cruz," said George. "Directly behind you. Then get in up here, next to me."

Cruz did as he was told, opened the rear door and threw the bag inside. He closed the door, and opened the front passenger door, stepped up and used the grab bar handle over the window to pull himself into the Range Rover. George sat next to him, a silenced Glock in his left hand, pointed across his stomach at Cruz. Cruz looked at the suppressor with a question on his face.

"Yes," said George, "this one is very short for a silencer, very convenient. It's an Aurora model, only about two inches long. Available to the US military only…and to Jefe, of course." George smiled with his mouth. He had not blinked since Cruz had looked at him through the open window.

"Put that on for our ride to see your daughter," said George, engagingly. A pair of handcuffs was hanging from the passenger's side grab bar over the door, one cuff connected to the grab bar, and the other awaiting a wrist. Cruz wrapped it around his right wrist and clicked until it was closed.

"Another click, please," said George.

Cruz complied.

George pushed his gun into Cruz's neck with his right hand, and with his left hand he patted down the passenger.

"Lean forward," he said. Cruz did. He had no weapon.

"Relax, Mr. Cruz, we're going on a short ride," said the Accountant as he pulled away from the curb. "Try to remain calm."

Cruz was silent.

CHAPTER 37

Kimmy had paused, leaned down, and opened the bedroom door in less than two minutes. Mary was behind her, waiting passively.

"Ok, so the trick here was to lever the lock a little bit, to sort of tease it back," Kimmy said. Mary nodded at Kimmy's back, as if she knew what Kimmy was talking about.

"We need to get you away from here," said Kimmy. "I'm not sure who that little man is, but I don't think he has good intentions toward you, Mary. Does this have something to do with Steve and all that mess?"

"I don't think so," whispered Mary. "I've never seen that guy before. He's totally creepy. Scares the hell out of me."

"Yes, I can see that," said Kimmy. They had made it to the galley kitchen, an open area in the rear of the home. "OK, here's the way out." Kimmy pointed at the back door.

* * *

The house was located in Dunwoody, a suburb about thirty minutes north of downtown Atlanta. From Olympic Park, George drove east on Andrew Young International Boulevard seven blocks to the Interstate overpass, and then took a left at the on-ramp north on I-85. The gun was an ever-present threat in George's lap; its nasty, deadly barrel pointing at Cruz's side.

Ten minutes later, at Brookwood, Interstate 85 turned gently to the east. George took that option. Less than three miles later, George exited north onto State Road 400, known locally as the Georgia Autobahn because of the overwhelming number of speeding cars that choose that particular route.

About seven miles of autobahn driving brought the Range Rover to the I-285 loop, and George exited onto I-285 east, then north onto Ashford-Dunwoody Road in Dunwoody, Georgia. A mile later, he turned the vehicle right on Valley View Road, and moments later turned into the driveway of an older home set back from the street with a large front lawn and mature oak trees. He pushed an opener, and the double garage door rose. George drove into the garage, the temporary door-opener light illuminating the space. He turned to Cruz.

"This is where your daughter is," he said.

* * *

"They're heading north," said Zeke as he watched the Range Rover access the downtown on-ramp to I-85 north. He was 200 feet behind in a dark green Honda Accord with Georgia tags. Sally and Clive were tracking him with the GPS on his smartphone. He turned left and followed the SUV.

"Alright, we go with the houses north of downtown," he heard Clive say to someone in the command room. Zeke's line was open and on the speaker at Clive's end. A moment later, Zeke heard someone talking with Clive in the background. And then, directed at the speaker, "There are four houses that we've identified in greater Atlanta, north of downtown," Clive said.

"Ok, I'll stay with him, and see if we can narrow it down as we go," said Zeke.

Zeke had followed the Range Rover on its way to Dunwoody. He and Clive had deduced that Cruz would most likely be taken to one of Jefe's drug houses and either killed or kept there until he could be taken elsewhere and killed. George's previous residence in the Omni hotel wasn't conducive to an execution, and there was nowhere in the midtown area that easily lent itself to loud noises and bloody deeds. Clive had also hidden a GPS device in Cruz's bag.

"Turning east on I-285," said Clive, apparently watching the GPS displays, and "that eliminates one of the four possibilities."

Zeke drove silently, working to keep the tan Range Rover in view.

"And that turn north you just made, onto Ashford-Dunwoody Road, eliminates two more houses, assuming that George is heading directly to his destination. That puts him at the house on Valley View Road, about two minutes from your present location. You may want to skip the turn onto Valley View, Zeke. It's a two lane, local road and you could easily be spotted."

"What's the address?" asked Zeke.

"The vacant house is 4337 Valley View Road," said Clive. It's set back from the road, a one-story with an attached double garage. Quite a number of trees around it, good natural disguise. And it has a long driveway, so they'll see anyone coming. It's owned by Jefe's brother, Enrique."

"OK," said Zeke. "I'll circle around the block and meet you nearby. You on your way?"

"You bet," said Clive.

* * *

George stepped out of the Range Rover into the garage and flipped the switch on the wall, which closed the garage door and turned on an auxiliary overhead light. The SUV was parked on the right hand side of the double garage. The left space was empty. The row of glass windows at the top of the double overhead door had been covered with white butcher paper, which had a translucent effect, yet it kept the interior of the garage invisible from the outside. George thought to himself that the use of butcher's paper was apropos.

When Jefe had offered this house to him, George understood the implications. Jefe wanted George to have a private place where he could do what he needed to do, without interruption. Implicit in that offer was the torture and slow death of Cruz, afraid and with no chance of escape. This house made the perfect location for such activities. That the women were also here was merely a bonus for George. He exited the Range Rover and circled around the rear to the passenger side, his silenced gun in hand. He opened the rear passenger door, and took out the duffle bag. Cautious as he always was, he circled back around to the driver's side of the SUV, dropped the duffle on the floor in the empty area next to him, and continued around the front of the vehicle. Then he stood near the right front headlight and leveled his handgun at Cruz. He was less than eight feet from Alberto.

On the garage wall on the rear of the house, the wall now facing the front of the SUV, two handicapped pull bars had been attached to the exposed two-by-four studs with heavy countersunk bolts. They were vertical, shoulder high, and about five feet apart.

George looked to the left side of the garage, the driver's side of the vehicle. There was an old workbench along the wall, with a pegboard above it and a few cabinets below it for storage. One of the cabinet's sliding doors was partially open, and George saw some scrap lumber and hand tools inside. A lawn mower and a red gas can were near the garage door entrance on that side of the garage.

On the other side of the garage, there was nothing but the interior wall about four feet from the car's passenger door. The wall was partially finished with drywall, to about five feet high, with studs and insulation showing above that.

"Mr. Cruz," said George, "please step out of the vehicle."

Cruz looked up at George with a question in his eyes. He looked at the handcuff on his right wrist, attached to the grab bar over the window and then back at the Accountant.

"Yes, open the door and slowly back out of the car. The

handcuff can stay in place," said George. "Or I can shoot you, and then go and shoot your daughter."

"Ok," said Cruz. "Ok." He pulled the inside door handle with his left hand and pushed the passenger-side door open with his foot. He slid down out of the passenger's seat and felt both feet on the smooth concrete of the garage floor through the slick soles of his dress shoes. He was facing back into the vehicle, with his right hand still attached to the grab bar.

George stepped forward to Cruz's right side, away from his free hand. With his gun still pointing at Cruz, George took another pair of handcuffs from his belt.

CHAPTER 38

Clive met Zeke in the Hobby Lobby parking lot, behind two pretty good chain restaurants. It was 7:20 in the evening, and both establishments were in full swing. The adjoining Walmart, however, appeared to be experiencing a slack period while most people were home, eating dinner.

Clive arrived in his two-year-old metallic gray Aston Martin Rapide S. He pulled into a parking space one away from Zeke and killed the engine. Zeke smiled and shook his head at Clive's traditional British tendencies. The car was a right-hand drive.

A moment later, Clive slipped into the front seat beside Zeke. "OK, let's go," he said.

"Taking my car?" said Zeke.

"Don't want to chance anything dicey with the Aston," said Clive, wryly. "There could be gunfire or something."

* * *

George tried the lock on the bedroom door and found it secure. He unlocked the deadbolt with his key and opened the door to the small room. In the darkened room, he could only make out shapes, but he was fairly certain there was no one there.

George pulled a small flashlight from his pants pocket and shone it around the room. All four walls, ceiling, closet space… nothing. There were two pairs of handcuffs and some used duct tape on the floor, along with the couple of small rags he'd used as gags, but that was all.

George closed the door and relocked it. He walked immediately back to the garage, cautious as he went, listening between steps. In the garage, George found things as he'd left them, with Cruz standing, his back against the reinforced back wall, arms spread and handcuffed to two vertical handicapped grip bars. He looked as if he were being crucified.

George leaned down, opened the duffle, and spilled out its contents. A large bundle of money hit the floor first, followed by some metallic cylinders wrapped in thick cotton cloth. They made a rather dull thud as they hit the ground. He opened one of the bags and confirmed that it contained counterfeit plates, as he expected. George put it all back in the duffle, threw the duffle back into the SUV, and looked at Cruz.

He had gagged Cruz earlier, before going back to the bedroom. "Mr. Cruz, open wide," George had said. He'd been holding a dirty rag in one hand, and the rest of the roll of tape in the other. He'd gagged Cruz quickly and secured the rag with two wraps of the tape around his head.

"I'm afraid that I must kill you now. Wait here while I

find your daughter. Then you can both die together," said the Accountant. "I won't be long."

* * *

It was likely that the women were still in the area, thought George, possibly even still in the house. He entered the house from the garage through the utility room and began a thorough search, room-by-room, door-by-door. It had gotten dark over the past hour, and there was little light inside the house. In each new room that he came to, George stood quietly with his eyes open for a moment, listening and feeling for any disruption in the air that may have been caused by sound or motion. A heartbeat, a breath, a movement would be all that he needed to distinguish a difference and isolate his prey.

George moved through the kitchen toward the small dining room, and he paused. He saw the back door in the kitchen, open slightly, but ignored it as a possible decoy. He continued through the living room and into the hallway. All was quiet.

George entered the master bedroom and stopped, waited, listened. No disturbance was evident. He looked in the small en suite bath, but no one was there. Returning to the hall, George checked the other bathroom, and then the third bedroom for the women. No one was present in the house. He could feel the absence of life there.

As a final thought, George went back to the prison, the modified bedroom with the boarded windows and open closet area. There was no one there either. The house was empty.

The interior search took 12 minutes, after which George exited the house through the back door, and searched the yard and surrounding area. He had found no sign of the women in the house, after a thorough and meticulous search. There was an area outside the back door where the grass had recently been matted down by footsteps. He could see the two different size footprints, both smaller, one barefoot and a women's size. The footprints went to the back of the yard and then into the foliage. There was pine straw on the foliage bed, and the tracks disappeared at that point.

This advances my schedule, George thought, as he returned to the garage.

* * *

"Mr. Cruz, your time has run out," said George. "Jefe wants you to understand what happens to those who defy his instructions. A lesson for you, and for others."

Cruz grunted into his gag. He saw that George had returned alone, which meant that Mary was safe…possibly. He could only hope.

"Do you see that drain in the center of the floor?" asked George. "There, to the side of the Range Rover."

Cruz saw it.

"It will be convenient." He took the large knife from his pocket. "I had planned to make this last all night," continued the Accountant. "An event that will cause fear for all of Jefe's adversaries. An event that will enhance my reputation even further. A devastating and overwhelming event.

"I was looking forward to hearing you beg, to hearing you plea for your daughter's life and then for your own. I've been looking forward to this evening of two slow, painful but related executions of Maria and then yourself.

"I had planned to hang your daughter from the beams in here," he said, pointing at several hooks and chains connected into the exposed support beams that crossed the open garage, "and I had planned to skin her. Flaying the skin from her muscle like you would a deer or a sheep.

"I prefer what is called 'Open Skinning', Mr. Cruz. I would first make a cut between her anus and her lower lip, right up the belly. And then I would make cuts up the inside of the legs and the arms. With that, the skin would peel away more easily.

"At first she wouldn't believe that it was happening to her, but soon she would see that there would be no recovery from such a thing. She would give up hope. That's the part I enjoy the most, Mr. Cruz. Looking into their eyes when they give up hope."

Cruz looked at him, shaking his head quickly.

"And by then I would have begun to cut her. I would have taken her fingers, one by one. And her ears, one then the other. And then her nose, and then her breasts. By that point she would have died a most unpleasant death, from shock or loss of blood or perhaps a heart attack. They always die by that point," he said fondly, almost to himself.

"But, it appears that we won't have the luxury of time, Mr. Cruz. We must be about our business."

The Accountant stepped up to Alberto Cruz, and, turning

sideways to avoid any thought of a kick, he deftly unbuckled Cruz's pants, ripped the zipper down and let them fall to the ground. Cruz was wearing white boxers.

The killer stared at Cruz with still, reptilian eyes, never blinking. "Your femoral artery is right there," he said, pointing with the sharp end of the knife. "It runs right along your thigh bone, most prominently at the middle and lower part of your thigh. When I slice it open, it will pump the blood from your body out onto the garage floor, and you'll bleed out in a minute or so. Long gushes of sticky red blood that smells like dirty copper."

Cruz shook his head frantically.

"There's no way to stop the arterial bleeding, Mr. Cruz. None. So, you'll know that you're dead before you pass out. You'll know that you're hopelessly dead, and there's nothing that can be done about it," said George.

"Right here," he said. He placed the knifepoint on Cruz's thigh. "Jefe sends his best. And be assured, your daughter will be next." George flicked his wrist deftly, cutting Cruz's thigh, and then he stumbled and fell.

CHAPTER 39

Clive and Zeke had parked the Honda three houses down from Jefe's house, in the driveway of what looked like a vacant house. There were no lights on in the house, and a metal "For Sale" sign was placed obviously in the front yard near the street. The lawn was a bit overgrown.

They circled the house and walked in the shadows to an area behind the house that County property records indicated was owned by Enrique Gurrerra. The house was dark and quiet.

Clive was dressed in matte black cargo pants, with a black tee shirt and matching cork-soled shoes and a black watch cap. He was essentially invisible as he moved through the yard. Zeke thought that he looked like some of the British Paratroopers he'd seen in James Bond movies.

The rear garage window was covered on the inside with a black plastic bag, and the rest of the house looked empty. Zeke and Clive made their way to the back of the house, and then quietly stepped through the partially open door into the kitchen. They moved from the kitchen into the small utility room, where they heard a quiet voice from the garage.

"Do you smell that?" mouthed Zeke. He sniffed again.

"No time," signaled Clive. He handed his silenced pistol to Zeke. "It's made ready," Clive said, moving his lips without volume. *British for 'cocked and locked'*, Zeke interpreted to himself. He palmed the gun and silently released the safety.

Clive's Browning Hi-Power MK III pistol was a throwback to his British Army days. Clive had carried that personal sidearm since Zeke had first met him about 7 years ago during Operation Iraqi Freedom. It was the prescribed British soldier's sidearm following World War II, and Zeke suspected it had replaced the more traditional basket-hilted claymore sword Clive had probably carried for years before that. This pistol was fitted with a suppresser.

Zeke quietly dropped to the floor and then quickly glanced around the corner of the doorjamb into the garage. The small man, George, was partially turned away from Zeke, up close with Cruz, and talking to him with an intimate tone in his voice. Zeke couldn't make out the words, but the sound was like a seductive whisper.

Left handed head shot, Zeke thought.

On his feet again, Zeke stepped halfway into the garage with his body perpendicular to George and Cruz, exposing as little of himself as possible. Arm extended, breathing out slowly, he braced against the doorjamb.

As George flicked his wrist at Cruz's leg, Zeke shot him in the right side of his head four times, the barrel of the MK III following George down to the floor. Pink puffs of vapor floated in the air, combined, and then fell to the ground covering the body. "Better than center mass," Zeke said to Clive.

* * *

"Bloody good shooting," said Clive from over Zeke's shoulder. The Accountant was huddled at Cruz's feet, a limp, lifeless pile of clothing, a headless body bleeding on Cruz's bunched pants and shoes. There was a lot of blood.

Zeke stepped into the garage, took a deep breath and cleared the space quickly. No one under or in the car, no one on the other side of the vehicle, Cruz now hanging from his handcuffs, leg bleeding slowly, eyes wide with terror, but also with recognition and therein, some hope.

"Let's get Mr. Cruz down," said Clive. He shut off the interior light and pushed the button to open the double garage door, knowing that the exterior glowing darkness that occurred just after sunset would provide them cover while they freed Cruz and cleaned up what was left of George.

Clive dragged George's body away from Cruz's feet while Zeke tied Cruz's leg with a towel tourniquet and began working on releasing Cruz's handcuffs.

"I suggest that you stand up straight and put your hands out to your sides. Or I'll shoot you," said Carlos, brandishing his AR-15 rifle.

Zeke relaxed away from Cruz, turned around and held his hands out from his sides.

"Drop the gun on the floor," said Carlos, and Zeke did, taking it from his belt and dropping it so it bounced off George's inert body to avoid an accidental discharge.

Clive released his hold on George's legs, and turned and looked at Carlos, his arms also held out from his sides.

"What other weapons do you have?" Carlos asked.

"I don't know what's in the car," said Zeke. "But my handgun is in the back of my belt," he said, knowing that Carlos had already seen it.

"Toss it down," said Carlos. Zeke set it on the floor gently and kicked it away. The gun slid across the concrete floor and came to rest near the workbench on the other side of the garage.

"It's loaded with hollow points," Zeke said to Carlos.

"Wait there," Carlos said. With his rifle aimed at them, Carlos looked around the garage and on both sides of the car. He glanced in the back seat and then walked over to the duffle bag on the floor.

"Jefe's counterfeit plates, I assume," he said, to no one in particular. He kicked the bag lightly and heard the muffled, padded metal sound.

Carlos pointed and Clive carefully took a small step to his right past Cruz toward the far corner of the garage and away from the door into the house. Carlos signed with his rifle barrel that Zeke should move that direction, also. Carlos stepped behind them toward the door to the house and pushed the automatic garage door button on the wall. The light came on and the garage door began to close, and Carlos stepped around the front of the car and then circled back to his left a bit, away from the car, improving his angle.

Carlos turned and said to Cruz, "You have run out of time. Jefe sent me to be sure nothing else goes wrong," he continued. "And it will not."

CHAPTER 40

After lying in the bushes at the back of the yard for what seemed like forever, Mary stepped through the pine straw and into the adjoining back yard. The back yards of the houses were wooded and dense, which provided good cover, but made for slower movement. She was barefoot and had to feel her way through the wooded area along the back fence, and across the property line to the neighboring house.

There was a light on, visible from the back of the neighbor's house and from the back of the yard Mary could see the flickering of the television set as its light came through the window. Through a smaller window, she saw a woman walk across what was probably the kitchen and turn out an overhead light. Mary stood still for a moment and listened for Kimmy behind her. She heard nothing but background noises, the tree frogs and the squirrels rustling. And then suddenly she heard a crack, like a loud whip, breaking the silence. It came from the house she'd just left.

* * *

As directed, Clive and then Zeke had carefully stepped farther away from the utility room and turned and waited for Carlos' next instruction.

"Sit on the floor, right there," he said. As Clive slowly moved to sit on the concrete garage floor, Carlos said, "I believe you know the potential of this AR-15. This one is set for a three-round burst mode right now. It is likely to kill you both with one pull of the trigger. We are, what, one meter apart?"

Behind Carlos, to his right, Zeke noticed a small movement in one of the cabinet doors under the workbench. The left side door panel slid open silently about six inches, and a small hand was framed in the opening.

"I have no time to waste, amigo," Carlos said as he moved to the right and knelt over George's body, quickly searching his pockets for the keys to the Range Rover. "I will take care of business and head back home." Carlos looked at the key fob with the Range Rover logo, nodded to himself and stood up. He moved to the left, back to where he was closer to Zeke and Clive, and he pointed the AR-15 at them.

In Carlos' mind, these men were already dead. He had seen movies in which the killer talked at length and explained to the victims what he was going to do and why. He'd seen TV shows where the killer went to great pains to be certain that the victim understood his motivations before he killed them. None of this made any sense to Carlos. All of the men before him would be dead in a few seconds. Why would he communicate with them now? It would be a waste of his breath.

In one fluid motion Carlos raised his rifle to head height, quickly leveling the barrel and sighting, and tightening his grip on the trigger as he prepared to execute Zeke and Clive. He had killed many men this way. He was already thinking about his exit and the duffle bag sitting on the floor.

Zeke stepped into the gunman, pushing the rifle barrel away to the left with his left forearm, grabbing the barrel and jamming the AR-15's sight into Carlos' eye with his right. Then there was a muzzle flash and a loud crack filled the silence of the garage.

From Zeke's vantage point, there was no result from the gunshot. And then a second later Carlos dropped the rifle and fell onto his knees. Carlos looked down in puzzlement, even disbelief, his eye bleeding from the blow from the rifle sight, and then he fell forward hard onto his face, his hands not breaking the fall. Zeke saw a small bloody hole between Carlos' shoulder blades, a perfect upper body mass shot with a hollow point bullet, which had inevitably bounced around inside his torso, tearing up all forms of organs, meat and bones. Carlos lay on the floor in a jointless heap.

"Got him," said Kimmy. She opened the small cabinet door under the workbench the rest of the way, and smiled at Zeke and Clive.

Clive was on his feet immediately, and while Clive disarmed the dying Carlos, Zeke helped Kimmy out of the small cabinet.

"How did you know I was hiding there," she asked Zeke, once she'd been extracted from the cupboard.

"I faintly smelled lilac when I first entered the utility room and the garage," he said. "I knew it wasn't from Cruz or George. Or from Clive. He's a D.R. Harris cologne man."

"Well, I'm glad you did," said Kimmy. "I wasn't sure what I was going to do. After I helped Mary get out, I decided to come back here and see what the kidnapper was planning. To see if I could help or something. And your comment about the hollow points gave me confidence to shoot him, even though you were in the line of fire. No chance of a through-and-through, Zeke," Kimmy said with a smile.

"Where is Maria? Where's my daughter?" said Cruz, when Clive removed the tape and the gag from his mouth. "Is she OK?" Cruz had a long cut across the front of his thigh, which was bleeding slowly down his leg. *No artery involved,* thought Zeke. Looks like George was enjoying it, taking his time and teasing Cruz.

"She's fine, Mary's fine," said Kimmy. "She went out the back door about ten minutes ago. I'd bet she's somewhere down the block, hiding. She couldn't be too far. She doesn't have any shoes on."

* * *

There was the usual commotion, with sirens and light-bars and floodlights and cops milling around everywhere. Zeke and Clive were detained in the back of separate Atlanta police cars while the house was searched and the supervisors tried to make sense of the scene. After the crime scene was marked off and the local policemen were posted to keep the neighbors away, Clive and Zeke were taken to the local police precinct, and each made their statement in separate rooms.

"Our role was accidental," explained Zeke, in an interrogation room at the police station. "We were looking at the house with the "For Sale" sign in front of it, and we heard some loud noises and decided to see if there was trouble."

"You just happened to be there at that moment?" asked Detective Black, a short heavy man with longish gray hair slicked back with some sort of hair oil. He smelled of Old Spice cologne.

"Yes, we did," said Zeke.

"You know it's a crime to lie to a police officer," said Black. He looked at Zeke with a cold eye.

Zeke nodded.

More cold-eye from Black.

Zeke tried to look nervous. He rubbed his hands together and looked away.

After Cruz had been uncuffed, Zeke and Clive conferred while Kimmy, bandaged his leg and kept a friendly eye on him. They decided that Kimmy should take Mary away from the crime scene. Any evidence of the women found in the bedroom prison or the house could be explained as being from an earlier time. If they did find evidence to track the girls, it would be almost impossible to find them. And, most likely DNA clues would take weeks to be confirmed. By then, a lot of things would have changed, beginning with their geography.

Detained as "persons of interest" at first, the evidence against

Zeke and Clive quickly began to organize itself into a legitimate self-defense situation. The fact that they had been facing an AR-15 rifle was in their favor. The fact that the two corpses were both known offenders, associated with the cartel and with history on the FBI's and the DEA's most wanted lists didn't hurt, either. And Clive's idea to put George's fingerprints on Zeke's handgun helped muck up the crime scene even further.

The Atlanta police quickly determined that Clive was a principal in The Agency, but at about the same time the local FBI office asked the police to release Clive and Zeke. Clive's recruiting skills were impressive. He had recruited a half-dozen highly ranked and respected former FBI agents to The Agency, who exerted their considerable influence on the Washington, DC Headquarters of the FBI, who in turn spoke with the FBI's Atlanta Special Agent In Charge, who immediately called the Chief of the Atlanta Police. Shortly after that phone call, Zeke and Clive were released, with stern warnings from Detective Black to "be available" and "don't leave town."

The witness to the shootings, Alberto Cruz, wasn't on the FBI's radar. He was a Mexican national with no record in the United States, and apparently none in Mexico. His fingerprints triggered nothing on IAFIS – the FBI fingerprint database – and calls to the Mexican Federal Police showed nothing of interest.

Mr. Cruz was reportedly a native of San Luis Rio Colorado, where he had no police record and no incidents with the local law. In interviews from his hospital bed, Mr. Cruz confirmed that both Zeke and Clive had saved his life, and that they had acted in self-defense.

Cruz further explained that he had been kidnapped by the small man and made to accompany him to this house. He expected that it was meant to be perhaps a robbery or a ransom situation, but it hadn't developed far enough to know.

CHAPTER 41

Riding with Kimmy in Clive's immaculate automobile, Mary was dialing her phone. Kimmy heard the distant ringing as she turned onto Highway 400.

"Hello?" said the tinny, male voice.

"What have you been doing?" asked Mary, almost hysterical with fright. "What were you thinking, Steve?"

"Whoa, wait, slow down, Mary. What're you talking about?"

"I'm talking about being kidnapped and almost killed, you bastard! You've been helping that madman, haven't you? He came and found me and said he was you! How could you?"

"Mary, what are you talking about?" was all that Steve could think of to say.

"Look, I've just been through the worst experience of my life, and I was almost killed by a short white guy who clearly knows you and used what you told him to..."

"Wait, Mary, a short white guy?"

"A sadistic short, white guy," she said. "You helped him, told him where I was, didn't you?"

"Oh, crap," said Steve. "How short?"

"Shorter than I am," said Mary.

"And he kidnapped you?" said Steve in disbelief.

"Handcuffs, a panel van, a gag, all the serial killer accessories, Steve. Did you think this would get us back together? No way, you moron. Just the opposite. I'm going to have you arrested!"

* * *

Clive spoke. "Apparently, Jefe has been buying up homes in larger US cities. From what Cruz told Tracy, Jefe buys a house and they keep it vacant, to use it as a shipping destination. They ship the drugs or counterfeit money FedEx to the vacant house, and then they watch the house to be certain there's no law enforcement in the picture. They watch some of these for a couple of days."

"From nearby?" asked Zeke

"They usually own a second house down the street that they use for observation," said Clive. "Ingenious, really."

"So you were looking for homes owned by some of Jefe's relatives, located on the same street or block," Zeke said.

Clive nodded.

"So we were right?" asked Zeke.

"Right. It appears that Jefe is diversifying his investments into real estate in some neighborhoods in this country," said Clive. "We were able to isolate the matches in Atlanta with little problem, once the Mexican Federales gave us the names and surnames of Jefe's family members. It just took a bit of time."

"I assume that Sally had a lot to do with that part," said Zeke, knowing he was on a secure line.

"She was right there the whole time," said Clive.

* * *

For the few remaining days until the court hearing for the disposition of property, Mary stayed with Kimmy again. Zeke and Clive approved the situation and considered the threat to Kimmy minimized, in that both George and Carlos were no longer in the game, and Steve had been arrested and was being detained by the Atlanta Police.

The arrest came after the Detectives investigating the multiple killings on Valley View Road were able to view George's smart phone, a burner that had been used to contact only three phone numbers. One of the numbers was from a local cell belonging to Steven P. Anderson, and the other two, in the 653 area code, were international phone numbers in Mexico.

Because of the several recent calls to and from Steve Anderson's number, a warrant was issued to search Steve's residence. A records search uncovered that there was a restraining order on a Steven P. Anderson of the same address, and that he was scheduled for a disposition of property hearing in Circuit Court in two days.

A senior Detective called the number from George's phone to gauge Steve's reaction. Steve answered, at which time diodes and transistors and towers and satellites all worked in concert to identify his location. After a brief conversation, Steve agreed to be interviewed. A Detective's car picked him up just ten minutes later at the house where he'd rented a room from a friend. Unfortunately for Steve, he was named as a person of interest, and spent the next few days with Atlanta's finest. And he missed the property distribution hearing.

Chapter 42

The hearing, for all of the anticipation, was anti-climactic. Mary was transported from Kimmy's apartment to the courthouse, and she and her attorney were ushered into the hearing by Zeke and Clive. The Sheriff's Deputy bailiffs had been alerted that they were coming and were already in place, in each corner of the hearing chamber. They each gave a short nod to Clive as he checked around the room visually.

As soon as the judge called the court to order, Steve's attorney requested a continuance.

"Your honor, my client isn't present today. We'd like to request that this Distribution of Property hearing be rescheduled for a time when he'll be available," said the attorney.

"Where is your client, Mr. Delacroix?" asked the judge.

"Approach, your honor?" asked Delacroix.

"Come on," said the judge.

The two attorneys approached the bench.

"Your honor, my client has been unfortunately detained by law enforcement in an unrelated matter," whispered the attorney. "He's being questioned by the Atlanta police."

"Your honor," injected Mary's attorney, Jack Tomlin, "although that is unfortunate, we do have a property distribution agreement that's been signed by both parties, and I see no reason to postpone this hearing. My client is anxious to get on with her life, and this hearing is the last in a series of steps to allow her to do just that."

"I've reviewed the agreement," said the judge. "Mr. Delacroix, I see no reason that I shouldn't rule on this matter now, even in the absence of your client. His signature is on the agreement."

Delacroix paused. "Mr. Anderson, my client told me that he was having some second thoughts about the property distribution. He wanted to contest some of the items in the agreement."

"Well, Mr. Delacroix, this is the third time that this hearing has been scheduled, and its been rescheduled by your client the last two times. I don't think that's particularly fair to Mr. Tomlin's client. In light of this signed agreement, I'm inclined to approve the agreement and put this matter to rest. As a matter of fact, I'm doing just that. Step back, please."

"Your honor," said Delacroix...

"The matter is resolved. I rule that the signed agreement be authorized by this court, and that the property be distributed as indicated therein immediately."

* * *

After the hearing, Clive and Mary returned to meet Zeke at his apartment. On the way, Zeke stopped by the hospital to chat with Alberto Cruz.

"Mr. Zeke, glad you stopped by," said Cruz. It sounded like he was back to his broken English.

"How's your leg?" asked Zeke, pointing. The bandaging was obvious; heavy white gauze had been wrapped around Cruz's thigh.

"Not, how do you say, not fatal," said Cruz. "Some stitches. I'll be OK in a few days. How is Mary?"

Zeke told him about Steve's detention and about the hearing. Cruz was apparently relieved. He sighed a long sigh and looked at Zeke.

"So she is OK now? No more threat to my Maria?"

"Mary is just fine, Alberto," said Zeke. "She's planning on leaving town soon, and I doubt Steve will have the time or energy to try to track her down. He's rather preoccupied, I gather."

"You saved me, amigo," said Cruz. "Not just me, but my daughter. I am most grateful to you and Mr. Clive for your efforts on our behalf."

"De nada," said Zeke. "It worked out. We ended up in the right place."

"Yes," said Cruz. "And now, they have me waiting here in this hospital. But the Secret Service agents haven't come to visit yet."

"I'm not certain if they've been informed of your participation in the activities the other night," said Zeke. "But I'll bet they do more than send flowers when they hear that you're here."

Cruz thought about that for a moment.

"Well, you know where to reach us if you need anything else, Mr. Cruz," said Zeke. "Thank you." Zeke left the hospital and headed back to his apartment.

CHAPTER 43

They were all sitting in Zeke's living room, looking out the large glass window overlooking downtown Atlanta and the slowly encroaching dusk.

"I believe that our work is done," Clive said to Mary. "We've delivered you safely, and you're done with the divorce hearing. Things might have gone a bit more smoothly along the way, but it's ended well."

"I think I'm good now," said Mary. "And the bad guys seem to have disappeared, at least for a while."

"They'll send more," said Clive. "Jefe can't be happy about losing the counterfeiting plates, or about Alberto escaping from George and Carlos. Plus, he's down a couple of his best guys now. A couple of specialists."

"It'll put a short-term dent in his operation, anyway," said Zeke.

"Well, I won't be waiting around," said Mary. "I'm packed and on my way south. Next stop, Calle Ocho."

"Your mother lives in Miami," said Zeke. "Are you planning to stay with her?"

"Only for a couple of weeks. Then, I'll move on to somewhere where no one knows me," she said, "just as you've suggested."

There was a knock at the door, and a moment later, Kimmy walked into the living area. "Hey," she said, and smiled. "How'd the hearing go? I was sending positive energy."

"Was the apartment door open?" asked Zeke.

"Oh, no, I saw you come back a little while ago. I just let myself in."

"Oh, you did, did you? Miss Show-off," said Clive.

* * *

Tracy Johnson was laughing. Sitting in the living room in Zeke's Midtown apartment, sipping a glass of Italian Merlot, she was sharing a story from her days in the Secret Service in Washington.

"So the suspect, he had to be close to three hundred pounds and was totally nuts, he tried to rush the White House, and got his head caught in the iron fence around the perimeter," she continued. "He was stuck there until we got a welder out to cut him loose."

Zeke smiled at the visual. After the others had left Zeke's apartment earlier, he and Tracy had met for a small plate dinner at a place near Tracy's office, and then walked together back to Zeke's. *The evening is going well,* he thought.

Tracy stopped talking and sipped her wine, looking at Zeke over her wineglass. *I could get lost in those eyes,* she thought again.

"I'm glad you came by," said Zeke. He noticed that Tracy's makeup was quite different from the last time he'd seen her. This time, it had been applied to accent her eyes and emphasize her lips and her long neck. She looked at him for a moment and nodded to herself.

Tracy set her wine down, stood up and walked over to the chair Zeke was sitting in. She put one hand on each of the chair's arms, leaned over and said, "I'll bet you're a great kisser."

Her eyes were just slightly dilated, and he swore to himself that he could sense pheromones in the air.

"Only one way to know for sure," he said with a smile.

She kissed him, and after a moment, he kissed her back gently. He tasted the subtle raspberry-plum flavor of the Merlot.

"Let's check out your bedroom," said Tracy. She seemed comfortable and animated.

"Sounds like fun," said Zeke.

Her skin was surprisingly soft and smooth to the touch, and yet beneath it her muscles were firm. Her green silk shirt was well fitted, but it came off easily. Naked, she slid her lithe body under the bed covers. Without her hair band, Tracy's thick hair fell free and framed her head on the pillow. She looked at Zeke lying next to her, and leaned in to kiss him again, this time hungrily.

For Zeke, the best part of this was the anticipation. *Go slow*, he thought as he kissed her again, nibbling her lip a bit and kissing her neck. She seemed to melt into him as he held her close gently, slowly learning the things that brought her best reactions. She had a lean body with long legs and an extended torso.

Zeke felt her smooth against his body, warm and comfortable.

"Fun is an understatement," she whispered. Zeke smiled.

* * *

"So tell me about Zeke," said Kimmy.

Clive and Kimmy were on their way to The Agency offices in Clive's Aston Martin. Clive was driving.

"Zeke's a lot like other people, I guess, but he has a gift of being able to physically sense more things than most people seem to sense," said Clive. "Like smells and sounds. He can feel temperature changes or light air movement and he can see very well, in the light or in the dark."

"That's a bit scary," said Kimmy. "Does he actually sense more, or has he just learned to not filter it?"

"Not sure, really," said Clive. "But because of this, his decision-making is generally based on more inputs than most people use. And he's been trained to try to use all of the available data around him to make the best decision at the time."

"That's useful," she considered.

"Combined with that, he's gifted with great coordination, both hand-eye coordination and full body coordination, which allows him to react quickly – and most of the time accurately – to situations. He's been trained to rely on the data or the inputs in a situation, and not on emotion or reactions," said Clive. "He seldom hesitates."

"I saw that," said Kimmy. "Very impressive."

"His memory is very good, almost eidetic, actually, and he

tries to keep it full of information that can contribute to his health and efficiency," said Clive. "He studies medical information, chemical composition of foods, the impact of our environment on our physical and mental health, that sort of thing. The goal is to maintain optimum efficiency while looking to extend his effectiveness over the years."

"And he certainly is fearless," she said.

CHAPTER 44

The Atlanta Police Precinct was a solid, brown brick building, reminiscent of what police precincts looked like in the last century, before the advent of creative architecture. There was probably a Civil Defense area in the basement, stocked with bottled water and medical supplies and sixty-five-year-old cans of food. Inside, the building was sparse and smelled of human sweat and dirty clothes.

"Are you sure we're supposed to turn this evidence over to you? The counterfeiting plates and the money?" asked the Desk Sergeant. He was a short, stocky man with thick black hair and stubble on his face that looked as if it needed shaving twice a day. His nametag read, 'Sergeant Crowley'.

"Yes, sir," said Ron, moving lightly to the high counter and showing his Secret Service identification. "Here's the paperwork." He handed it to the policeman.

"Let me check, OK?" said Crowley. He picked up the desk phone and turned away from Ron and Tracy. A short conversation ensued. Crowley shook his head, then nodded, and finally hung up with a "Yes, sir."

"It's yours," he said to the space between Ron and Tracy, and he went back to the important papers he had been reviewing on his desk. Tracy recognized them as a personnel schedule.

"OK, thanks," said Ron. He took the two large, sealed plastic evidence bags off the desk and walked out the door. Tracy followed him.

"Glad to be out of there," said Tracy. "I think you can pretty much tell the crime rate of an area by the smell of its precinct house." They got into the Crown Vic they'd parked in front of the building in a "Police Only" spot and drove back toward downtown.

Earlier in the week, Clive had called and informed the Secret Service of the location of the missing printer plates with the Atlanta Police and shared that Cruz was recovering from his wound in the hospital.

Tracy dialed Fitch from the car.

"We've got them, boss," she said. "Heading back in."

Fitch sounded irritated. "OK, good. Let's get them in here and locked up."

"On our way, boss. What's up?"

"Looks like we've lost Mr. Cruz again is all," said Fitch, tightly.

"What? How?" asked Tracy. She switched the cell phone to speaker mode.

"He's gone. He got up, got dressed, and walked out of the hospital!"

* * *

Clive was sitting at a two-top table near the polished wood bar in Meehan's Public House next to the Westin Hotel in downtown Atlanta. It was two short blocks from Luckie Street and a half block off of Andrew Young International Boulevard. Meehan's is an authentic Irish Pub with wide plank dark wood floors, an open ceiling and stained glass appointments. Booths are arranged along one wall, with floor to ceiling dividers that assure some level of privacy. Clive was sipping a martini made with Sipsmith's traditional London Dry gin, which he favored for its smoothness.

"This is one of the few places that you can get this around here," said Clive, gesturing with his left hand to include all of Atlanta or perhaps all of Georgia. It was hard to tell. "Good stuff."

"You didn't tell me about the back-up," Zeke said. There was an ice-cold glass in front of Zeke.

"Didn't know about it specifically," said Clive. "We hired Kimmy – her name is actually Tzofiya, pronounced a bit like Sophia, but spelled all kinds of weird – The Agency hired her as a backup for the Cruz exchange. Strictly background, for observation and communications. Apparently, she was, well, enthusiastic, and got closer to you than we expected. I had no idea, old man."

The waitress approached and looked over questioningly, and Clive waved her over. "Hungry?" he asked.

"Sure," Zeke said and picked up a menu.

"Bangers and Mash," said Clive. "And a pint of Guinness with it, if you please."

"Brilliant," said Zeke quietly, with a smile to himself. And to the waitress, "I'd like a grilled tuna sandwich, please. With cheddar cheese, on wheat bread."

She noted the orders, nodded and turned away.

"Sally set it up with Kimmy," Clive continued. "She's former Mossad, you know, Israeli Secret Service. They're a competent lot."

"So Kimmy was supposed to be my backup in case of trouble," said Zeke. He was sipping a black and tan, and was seated facing the bar and the front entrance of the pub. Clive had an excellent view of the rear of the place.

"I figured it out, actually," said Zeke. "That's why I let Mary stay with her."

"How did you know?" asked Clive.

"A number of little things," said Zeke. "And the way she carried herself, her attitude, her confidence. Plus her Star of David tattoo and the fact that she was Israeli…things like that."

"Well, we set that up through The Agency," said Clive. "She's an operator with wet work experience and she came with a hearty recommendation from a personal friend of mine, a fellow still in the business. Thing is, she changed her name to 'Kimmy' and I never saw her at your apartment, so we weren't aware that she'd moved in next door to you."

"Across the hall," said Zeke. "She must have learned where I was moving from Sally and then rented an apartment a day before I got there. And she was slick, always around keeping watch on me, getting involved in my situations. It was very well done."

"I'm told that all Israelis are required to spend two or three years in the military when they turn 18," said Clive, "three years for men and two for women. I'd think she spent more than two years, and they were probably spent in Israel's version of MI-6."

"In the end, I was glad she was there," said Zeke.

"Actually, her name means 'guardian,'" Clive said. "As you've probably figured, I've offered her a permanent position with The Agency," said Clive.

"I'd expect no less," said Zeke. "She certainly earned it."

"My offer to you still stands, too, Zeke. Will you consider coming aboard full time?"

"I'm flattered, Clive. But I think I'd rather come in when you really need me. I think I'm getting too independent to be available all of the time. I'm enjoying the in-between times more and more."

"And that defines you, my friend. The one I call for only the most dangerous situations. The specialist."

There was a pause in the conversation. "Well, what about the elephant, then?" asked Zeke.

"Ah, yes," said Clive. "Jefe. He's still out there and dangerous, you know."

"How about the Secret Service?" asked Zeke. "Are they still in pursuit?"

"They're not authorized to operate outside of this country," said Clive. "Nor is the FBI. They have to work through the Mexican government, and that's not going very well."

"Simple corruption," said Zeke. "At least enough to tip Jefe off when someone gets close.

"And, as strange as it seems, Jefe's operation is too small to draw the kind of attention that would interest your CIA. So, that leaves...us."

"Right.

"We're already halfway into it," said Clive. "I can't see any reason for us to stop now."

"I know," said Zeke. "Seems a shame to leave it unfinished. And I'm not one who favors watching my back all the time."

"Right. So, to the larger mission," said Clive, as he lifted his glass.

CHAPTER 45

"Colonel David Finester speaking," said the voice.

"Commander of Task Force Leatherneck?" asked Zeke. "Have you been back to Afghanistan since that operation?"

"I'm afraid that's classified," said Finester with a smile. "You can read about it in the newspapers. 'Operation Enduring Freedom- Afghanistan', they called it."

"Great to hear your voice again, Dave," said Zeke.

"And yours, Zeke. What have you been up to?"

"Well, I retired from MICECP a couple years ago..."

"Yes, I remember hearing something about that."

"...and went private contract. I've done a few jobs with Clive Greene. You remember Clive, I'd guess," said Zeke.

"Can't forget Mad Jack," said Finester.

"Right," said Zeke. Clive Greene was often compared with Mad Jack Churchill, a British officer in World War II who once took a group of twenty-six German soldiers prisoner with only his sword and a single fellow officer. His bravado as well as his eccentricities were legendary.

"The counterintelligence you guys supplied in Afghanistan made the Battle of Marjah a cakewalk for our guys."

"Yeah, that worked out pretty well," said Zeke.

"You have a knack for that, as I recall. Sorry to hear that you're out of it now."

"Well, not totally out of it. I'm just able to pick and choose my operations now. With the terrorists so prevalent, none of us can afford to retire."

"So if you're not working for the Army, does that mean you're no longer active in our Marine Corps Martial Arts Program training? Or the Invitationals?" said Dave.

"No longer," said Zeke. "But those were good times. I always enjoyed the Corps Judo tournaments."

"You always enjoyed winning the Corps Judo tournaments, you mean," said Finester wryly.

"Listen, we've come across a little something that I think may interest you, Dave. It's a parallel track to an investigation we've just wrapped up."

"OK," said Finester.

"There was a Gunny in your command named Lopez. He was a standout. Manny Lopez. I seem to recall that he won the Navy Cross."

"I remember Gunny Lopez. He's been out for a while."

"Yes, sir. After he left the Corps, he became a cop. He worked in Phoenix for about three years, and then he moved back home to Mexico. Apparently, his mother was living in San Luis Rio Colorado. The locals call it Sonora Rio."

"Where's that?" asked Finester.

"Just south of Yuma, Arizona," said Zeke. "Just over the border."

"OK," said Finester.

"He moved back and took the Chief of Police position. You remember Lopez. He was always sticking up for the innocent, trying to make things right. I think the situation in San Luis Rio Colorado ground on his sense of right and wrong. He was hearing about it from his mother all the time. So, he moved back to try to set things right."

"That's Mexican Cartel territory, isn't it? Illegal immigrants and drugs and counterfeiting and such?"

"Some of the worst," said Zeke. "So Manny went back home to clean it up. Like a Mexican 'Walking Tall' story."

Finester let a low whistle escape his lips. "Shit," he said.

"Yeah, it didn't take long. They shot him about 30 times with AK-47's. He was off duty and at home. Got in his car to go to the store and they followed him and killed him. I'm sorry."

"I am, too," said Finester. What a waste."

* * *

The rain was pouring down, and the wind was blowing it almost sideways into Zeke's picture window. Visibility was limited to about two gray yards. Occasionally, lightning bolts would light up the downtown sky, revealing high-rise buildings and interstates in the distance.

"I spoke with one of my FBI contacts," said Clive. "They liaise with the Mexican law enforcement on joint projects. Since

Guzman escaped from jail, the Mexican government has been under a lot of pressure to cooperate with the FBI and the DEA."

"No doubt," said Zeke. They were sitting in the living area of Zeke's apartment, Clive on the couch and Zeke in a chair across from him, and Kimmy on a stool at the island in the kitchen. Both Kimmy and Zeke were drinking coffee, Clive was sipping tea, and the coffee table was spread with notes and papers and notebooks and Pads. They were in their planning mode.

"So, the FBI has agreed to instigate a joint raid on Jefe's compound in San Luis Rio Colorado," said Clive. "They'll have to run it through the right channels and coordinate it with the right agencies, but my guy says that the Mexican government is desperate to show that they're proactive in fighting the drug cartels. So, with a bit of a push, they'll set it up. Our guys will be 'advisors.'"

"They've raided Jefe's compound before," said Kimmy. "What happened those times?"

"He's always escaped," said Clive. "The popular theory is that he's usually been tipped off by someone in the police or government and has been able to escape before the federal police can contain him. His resources are pretty vast, and he's not afraid to run away and come back to play another day."

"So, how will this be different?" asked Kimmy.

CHAPTER 46

"Jefe," he said, announcing himself on his cell phone.

"They'll be coming pretty soon, Jefe," said the deep voice in Spanish. "The agents from the United States FBI and DEA are already here, in Mexico City. They are planning the raid."

"When?" asked Jefe.

"No more than three days, Jefe. They all talk about their budgets and resources and the need to move quickly, and to get results."

It had been more than three weeks since Carlos had been dispatched to Atlanta and Jefe's informants in the Mexican Federal Police had been giving him status reports every other day. This was the culmination of several weeks worth of advanced effort, and it sounded like a raid was eminent. *Too much pressure by the US government,* he thought.

The blazing heat of the summer in Sonora Rio had eased a bit over the past few weeks, and the blistering temperatures were more bearable during the autumn days. Still, Sonora Rio was dusty and hot and dry and unpleasant. Jefe thought about his island home for a moment.

"How many are involved?" asked Jefe to the man on the phone.

"There are about 75 people in total, including the agents and the technicians and the soldiers." By "soldiers" he meant those with guns, those who would lead the raid on Jefe's home.

"Very well, then, thank you," he said quietly, and hung up. *This calls for a quick and decisive action*, Jefe said to himself. *There is no time to waste.*

The loss of George was an inconvenience, but the loss of George and Carlos at the same time had a somewhat crippling effect on his organization. It took away options that he needed right now.

Carlos had been Jefe's personal guard and a ranking lieutenant in the organization. But also, he was an enforcer, and he was a pilot, usually the co-pilot on Jefe's Learjet. He was trustworthy. He had been with Jefe for many, many years. Their children played together, and their wives shopped together. He was as close to a friend as Jefe had.

Consequently, things had slowed some over the past few weeks, and Jefe was still looking for the right replacements for Carlos in his various capacities.

When Jefe bought his Learjet, he paid extra to have Carlos trained to fly it. The peace of mind that came with knowing that Carlos was double-checking the pilot's every move and was in a position to stop anything that might not be in Jefe's best interest made the investment in those lessons worthwhile. Carlos had had a commercial pilot's license, and the additional Learjet training added a layer of security to an unsecure situation.

Several years ago, on the Caribbean Island of Grand Cayman,

Jefe had purchased a home. It was a large and sprawling mansion with views from every room, a private beach and security on all sides. The house was located not far from the airport, on South Sound Road in George Town, and had cost Jefe about twenty million dollars at the time he bought it.

It was built on two oversized lots, which allowed for a four-car garage, a full-size tennis court and a large pool. Views of the Caribbean Ocean were visible from virtually everywhere in the house and from all of the outdoor space. The living area was built of dark wood and marble, with 24-foot trey ceilings that allowed for floor to ceiling windows on the south, ocean-front wall. Jefe quickly had the windows replaced with bullet-proof glass.

There were automatic window shutters on each window, which would protect the home in case of an errant storm. There was an enclosed widow's walk on the roof, accessible from interior stairs. It doubled as a guard's tower. The staff Jefe hired consisted of fifteen people, half locals, who took care of the kitchen, yard, pool, tennis court, house maintenance and housekeeping. Jefe relocated the other half of the staff, taking with him trusted family members and a part of his security team, some of whom moved into the servant's quarters, and a couple of whom travelled between this house and Sonora Rio with Jefe.

The entire compound was retrofitted with armor-plated protection, all the locks were updated to the current state-of-the-art, and the security system was replaced with the best protection that money could buy. Jefe had a lot of money.

The home was secure electronically as well as physically, and its location along a populated strip of beachfront acted to prevent more serious military action against Jefe. An armed force that approached, either from the sea or the road, would have to consider collateral damage to his neighbors and their families, as would those who might launch a drone attack on the villa. Early warning systems were in place, and in addition to the multiple safe rooms, there were two escape tunnels secreted in the compound.

The famous Seven Mile Beach was located just on the other side of George Town, where various cruise ships came and went several times each week. And Jefe kept his yacht moored at the tony George Town Yacht Club.

The government was perfect. The Cayman Islands actively encourages high net worth individuals to obtain residency, in a tax neutral environment. The Cayman Islands have no local taxes at all. And the Caymans have no extradition agreement with any other country. Jefe smiled when he thought about that.

"It is probably time for a trip to the Caribbean," Jefe said to no one in particular.

* * *

The Learjet 75 sat proudly on the tarmac, glistening in the Sonora sun. With a cruising speed of just over 500 miles per hour, and a range of just over 2,000 miles, the aircraft could easily get to Grand Cayman with one stop to refuel. Typically, that stop was at the Monterrey Airport. The Corpus Christi

International Airport was actually a shorter route, but Jefe felt that the extra time was worth it, in order to stay in Mexican territory for the entire trip over land. After the planned stop in Monterrey, the journey to Grand Cayman was 1,300 miles, well within the range of his jet. It was usually a smooth, comfortable ride east to his oceanfront home. He thought of it as his vacation home.

At the airport, the pilot approached Jefe. "Carlos isn't flying with us?" he asked in Spanish. It was a polite question. He had heard the rumors of Carlos' death in Atlanta.

"Not today, Raul," said Jefe. "Did you find a replacement co-pilot?"

"Si," said the pilot. "It was short notice, but I was able to call the Learjet people, and they were able to recommend a pilot who was in the area…he flew in from Phoenix yesterday."

"And he's checked out on the Model 75?" asked Jefe.

"He is, he was given a good recommendation by the aviation people at Learjet. He's been licensed commercially for fifteen years, and they said he worked as a substitute on Air Force One for George Bush, Jr.," said the pilot. He felt that was an excellent recommendation. "He told me that his mother was Cuban, and he speaks fluent Spanish."

Jefe smiled at the irony. "OK, good," he said. "Keep an eye on him and be sure he knows what he's doing."

"Si, Jefe," said the pilot.

"We'll leave this morning, as soon as my staff arrives," said Jefe. "Maybe an hour."

"Si, Jefe," said the pilot. "We'll be ready."

CHAPTER 47

"How long do you think we'll be staying in the islands, Antonio?" asked Gabriela, Jefe's wife. She used his given name.

"I'm not sure. A couple of months, probably," he said.

"Oh, good," said Gabriela. "Its so nice there, so peaceful and beautiful."

"I think I'll take the boys fishing," said Jefe. "We should go out for Blue Marlin or Tarpon."

Gabriela was sitting next to Jefe in one of the four seats closest to the rear of the plane. The seats in the next row forward were reversed, two of them looking through the plane to the tail area. The front row faced forward. All of the seats were occupied.

Between the second row and the third row were tables, allowing passengers to talk in small groups and to spread out their possessions. The airplane was designed for a comfortable ride, with luxury detailing to enhance the experience. The refueling in Monterrey was uneventful, and after stretching their legs, the party boarded the plane again, took their same seats and buckled their seatbelts.

The copilot's voice came over the Bose speakers in quiet Spanish. "We're on course and should be arriving at the Owen Roberts International Airport in Grand Cayman in two hours and twenty-five minutes. The weather is clear on our route and we expect an uneventful flight."

The best kind, thought Jefe.

* * *

Exactly three hours later, the copilot's voice came over the speakers again. "We've been cleared to land. Please take your seat and be sure that your seatbelt is buckled. We'll be on the ground in a few minutes."

Jefe took his seat while Gabriela helped their two children get seated and buckled in. His two bodyguards also buckled in. Out the starboard window, the Caribbean Sea was bright blue and the sun was shining overhead.

Jefe glanced at his Patek Philippe watch and noted that they had made poor time to Grand Cayman, arriving behind schedule. He chalked it up to the new co-pilot.

Shortly thereafter the plane touched down gently and rolled to the end of the tarmac. Jefe looked out the window at the buildings as they rolled past the runway.

"Wait, what is this? Where are we?" Jefe asked one of his men. The man looked puzzled.

Jefe picked up his microphone and toggled the switch. "Raul, where are we?" he asked the pilot.

There was no answer. The Learjet turned and taxied back

toward the terminal building and radar tower, and then slowed to a stop on the tarmac. Out of the window, Jefe saw four armored personnel carriers with U.S. Marine insignias on them turn the corner of the terminal building, moving quickly toward the plane.

"Raul, what's going on?" asked Jefe into the microphone. "Where are we?" He got up from his seat, took his Glock from its holster and went to the cockpit door.

With the armor-plated door to the pilot's area secured from the cockpit side, it was virtually impenetrable. Airplane design had been updated since 9/11 to prevent hijacking and terrorists seizing control of an aircraft. As on commercial flights, once the cockpit door was closed, it was secure.

Still hearing no response from Raul, Jefe pounded on the door with the butt of his pistol while each of the Marine Personnel Carriers took a position around the plane. Each carrier aimed its attached .50 caliber machine gun directly at the Learjet.

Start to finish the action took about one minute. The first Marines dispatched from the MPC's quickly put chocks and locks on each tire, assuring that the plane would remain in place. The second wave of men deployed from each vehicle were wearing full battle gear, helmets and vests, and were carrying semi-automatic assault weapons. They surrounded the Learjet as stairs were advanced to the exterior cabin door. When they were in position a few short moments later, there were thirty-two Marines circling the airplane, with thirty-two semi-automatic rifles pointed at it.

Jefe heard the engines slow and stop. There was no response

from the cockpit. He turned back into the cabin.

A speaker located on the personnel carrier closest to the stairs came to life. "Open the door and deplane," said an authoritative voice in Spanish. "Put your weapons down and exit the plane. Walk down the stairs backwards, one at a time. Do it now!"

* * *

"You can't do this," Jefe was saying to the Marine Sergeant, a large black man who was apparently in charge of the action. Jefe was seated in a small locked room in a brick building near the tarmac, handcuffed and shackled and surrounded by three very muscular and very serious Marines. They had been waiting for a few minutes.

"There is no extradition agreement between Grand Cayman and any other country, particularly not the United States," said Jefe. "You can't hold me here."

His family members and his men had been separated and taken to holding cells as they exited the plane.

"Actually, my friend, we're on American soil. And so, we can hold you, and we can hold you accountable for all that you've done," said the Sergeant.

"What are you saying?" asked Jefe.

There was a sharp knock on the door. Then Zeke walked into the room, wearing a short-sleeved co-pilot's shirt with epaulets and a captain's hat. He smiled at Jefe and said in Spanish, "Welcome to Guantanamo Bay, Senor Jefe."

CHAPTER 48

"Executed with flair, old boy," said Clive. "Nicely done."

Zeke smiled. They were sitting in a small conference room in Clive's Agency offices in Washington, DC. The table was made of blond wood and the chairs were comfortable leather with swivels and wheels. The large window on one wall looked out over Pennsylvania Avenue and, ironically, the Department of Justice building.

"How did you know Jefe would run to the Caribbean?" asked Kimmy.

"My contacts at the FBI and DEA were spot on," said Clive. "They've tried the joint raids before with the Mexican officials, and each time Jefe was tipped off, and each time he flew his plane to Grand Cayman. They've been watching him but just couldn't get to him quickly enough. I think they're happy with these results, though."

"It didn't hurt that Colonel Finester had the right contacts at Gitmo," said Zeke. "And it didn't hurt that Marines never leave one of their own behind. Especially not one who won the Navy Cross."

"Right," said Clive. "And now that the Marines have Jefe in a Guantanamo Bay cell, and they know that he ordered the murder of Manny Lopez, the ex-Marine and Police Chief in San Luis Rio Colorado, I'm guessing that Jefe will disappear off the grid, like a Bermuda Triangle sort of thing. Some of those terrorists at Gitmo have been there for years."

"Either that, or they'll take him stateside to stand trial and serve his time there," said Zeke.

"How did you make that happen?" asked Kimmy.

"It was a good plan," said Zeke. "Finding that Carlos was checked out as a co-pilot on Jefe's plane was key. The FAA card that we found in Carlos's wallet in the garage led to that, and without Carlos, I figured that Jefe would have to find a replacement co-pilot for his escape to Grand Cayman. The raid on his compound in Sonora Rio was the instigator to make him run. After that, he was pretty predictable. And he was contained."

"How did you get the co-pilot position, Zeke?" asked Kimmy.

"Clive used his contacts with the FBI to get the Learjet people in Kansas to recommend me as an available pilot, cleared to fly the 75 model, and proximate to Sonora Rio. Actually, I believe they were waiting for the inquiry from Jefe's man, Raul. There aren't many commercial pilots checked out on that equipment that are immediately available."

"And you are checked out on it?" asked Kimmy.

"Well, I had to do some quick study, but it turned out well," said Zeke. "Once we were in the air out of Monterrey, it was simple to incapacitate the pilot and take control."

"And you just landed in Cuba instead of Grand Cayman?"

she said. “Sounds simple.”

“Not simple. But the Marines set up all of the permissions with the Cuban military, and they changed the flight plan once we were in the air. My part was to set her down and to deliver Jefe.”

“What happens now?” asked Kimmy.

“I suppose that eventually someone will take over Jefe’s spot in the cartel and it’ll be business as usual,” said Clive. “But we did what we could for our client. I don’t think Alberto will need to look over his shoulder any longer. Nor will we.”

CHAPTER 49

After Labor Day the crowds in Florida slack off for the shoulder season, the "in-between" fall season, before returning with a vengeance beginning in mid-December and continuing through the late spring. Zeke chose this particular barrier island because the coming and going of weekly and monthly guests promised a polite privacy and provided for acceptable social distancing. And social distancing was his goal.

For Zeke, last summer had been busy with a complex recovery operation in Turkey that ended well, but took more time than he'd expected. And in September, he had worked with Clive Greene in Atlanta. So he'd been looking forward to days made up of morning workouts and afternoon sunshine combined with occasional research and a spot of exploration. This particular tourist destination, Marie Island, is popular with Europeans and Canadians who tend to favor the south and west sides of the Sunshine State. When the Euro is strong against the weaker dollar, the cottages on this Florida Island are booked solid.

"Did you have any other questions, Zeke?" Mrs. Skilowicki asked. "There's a map in the basket on the counter. The Wi-Fi password is taped to the router."

Mrs. Skilowicki, the woman Zeke was renting from, was a Tampa resident. She was delighted to have a rental longer than a week or two, and she was very accommodating in helping him get oriented to the property and the area. Negotiations were held over the phone and via e-mail and he'd called her when he arrived at the cottage.

"No, I'm probably good," he said into the phone. He'd found the rental early in his search and secured the cottage for four months, beginning the first weekend in October. From his previous rental experiences he knew that after school is back in session demand wanes a bit in most tourist locations. The four-month rental of a third row cottage between October and January was both attractive and lucrative to vacation home landlords. And he knew that paying in advance for the entire visit – at full price – certainly sweetened the deal.

It was his preference to rent, not buy, and Zeke chose to live in transient areas like this one. In the neighborhoods he frequented, short-term guests are common, and the locals begrudgingly accept them as a necessary evil. Their presence keeps the shops and restaurants in business during the off-season.

Mrs. Skilowicki said, from the other end of the phone line, "The washer and dryer are in the second bathroom closet, and you'll find beach chairs and all that in the garage. The kitchen has most of your staples, salt and pepper, sugar, coffee, that sort of thing. We just ask that you replace what you use when you leave."

He thanked her and signed off, promising to contact her if he had any questions. *I'm a bit old fashioned in some ways,* he thought. *Some might say that I'm overcautious.*

Zeke stepped out on the front porch and into the small yard and looked around. The neighborhood of cottages had a quaint feel to it, and there were people in swimsuits all around the area, carrying chairs and beach bags and coolers to and from the beach access. He dialed his phone.

"Tracy Johnson," she answered.

"Hey, Tracy, I was just thinking about you," Zeke said.

"Really, why's that?" she asked with a light tone in her voice.

"Well, I was wondering whether you're in another relationship yet," he said.

"Hmm. Tell me, am I?" she teased.

"Seems like you could be heading in that direction," Zeke said. "I was also wondering if you have any vacation time coming?"

* * *

The cottage itself was painted a bright yellow with white trim and sky blue accents. There was a long porch across the front of the building, which looked out onto the gravel driveway and the two-lane street that led to the beach. There was a flowerbed in front of the porch dotted with aloe and hibiscus plants and there was one lone palm bush near the side property line.

Inside, the property was functional, although it had some age on it. The front door led past the kitchen to the open dining and living area. It was a good space with a wall of windows on the back, overlooking a small swimming pool and a fenced yard. Beyond the fence was an alley, also of gravel, that extended along a drainage easement for the entire block. The cottage had high ceilings and several large fans actively cooling the living areas.

To the left Zeke saw a small hallway that led to the bedrooms and bathrooms. The décor in the living area was primarily "old conch," a flavor of the Keys and Key West. The colors were pastels and the paintings were watercolors of beach scenes and boat docks and fish. There was a garish, wall-eyed tarpon mounted over the television set in the living area.

Zeke sat back in a tan leather club chair and found it to be pretty comfortable. The overstuffed sofa looked less so, but he was sure it'd be fine for a few months. The sofa was a beige and green pattern, and matched the wall color, a pastel green with beige trim. One wall was covered in mirrors, to make the place look larger than it was. It was a nice effect, but for just one person he didn't need a lot of space. Zeke tended to blend comfortably into his surroundings.

He usually lived alone, and that lent itself well to smaller, one- or two-bedroom cottages. Typically a bike was the most practical transportation, or perhaps a short walk. Zeke kept his old BMW with him, but he seldom took it out of the garage.

And there were some other advantages to this life style. His housing came fully furnished, which saved him the trouble of moving furniture or replacing things as they wore out. Maintenance was taken care of by the owner, and in seaside locations, which he tended to select, the wear and tear of the salt and the sand increased the need for ongoing maintenance.

This cottage met all of his criteria, with two-bedrooms and two-baths, a small porch area, a short walk to the white sand and blue water, 361 days of sunshine each year – according to the Chamber of Commerce – and a constant surf temperature of 80 to 84 degrees in the summer. According to the Internet, there were a couple of local restaurants near the water that served highly rated fish sandwiches, and the island was in reasonable proximity to McDill Air Force Base for his quick transport, if necessary.

CHAPTER 50

Moving around a few times a year tends to accentuate the similarities of places, as opposed to the differences. Having been pretty much self-contained for the past ten years, Zeke had been able to fine-tune his perceptions. *I'm probably self-contained in my opinions, too,* he thought.

There are about twenty things that all of us do. And of those twenty, about six are discretionary. The rest are pretty much mandatory, for most people. Eat, sleep, work, pay bills, like that. That's part of the thought process that made Zeke change his lifestyle a few years back.

Zeke describes what he does as "real-time problem solving in three-dimensions." He enjoys quickly processing the available data and information to make fast decisions and take action. It's somewhat like judo, as you have to feel the subtle shifts in weight and balance and respond immediately once your opponent has committed himself. It's often a tense and demanding occupation, and what downtime Zeke gets is a welcome respite.

One of the first things Zeke does when he moves to a new

location is to look for a local dojo for Judo practice. It's not unusual to find such a place, primarily aimed at teaching kids the martial arts, but with a sensei who has the skill set to be a challenging opponent on the mats. On this island, Zeke had spotted Island Dojo Martial Arts. It advertised a prowess in the popular art of Brazilian Jiu Jitsu. *That's perfect,* he thought to himself.

Beach volleyball had also become a part of Zeke's fitness routine. Admittedly, Zeke generally played on teams with four people on each side of the net, and with deep sand and hot sun, a couple or three sets makes for a pretty good workout. This year he'd been feeling like he may have lost a step, and the volleyball court just down at the beach from Mrs. Skilowicki's cottage – well, his cottage, now – looked like a promising way to get that step back.

A ball in his beach bag just in case, along with a towel, some low level sunblock and a bottle of water, Zeke walked down to the beach. He set his bag down in the sand a respectful distance from anyone else and sat in the sand next to it. He found that he was particularly fond of locations that attach more importance to the local tide table and the moon phases, than to clocks. *This place qualifies,* he thought.

The beach sand was bleached white, whiter than most other places in this country. There were some sunbathers lying on towels scattered about and a handful of visitors who had brought their own chairs, generally clustered in small groups of two or three. A couple of them had brought beach umbrellas. At a concrete picnic table under a nearby tree, Zeke spotted two older men playing chess. *Oh, good,* he thought, *chess games.* The gulf breeze was pleasant, maybe seven to ten knots, just enough to keep the flies away and to cool the early October heat. So far, he liked it all.

Zeke turned to look toward the ocean. There were small waves, and the sun glimmered off the blue water. There's a therapeutic effect associated with proximity to the ocean, and he was starting to feel it already.

* * *

Zeke had picked Tracy up at the Tampa Airport after her direct flight from Atlanta. She had one carry-on with her when they climbed into his BMW, parked in the short-term lot.

"What's in that?" he asked her. "Swimsuits?"

"I didn't think I'd need much," Tracy said, looking directly at Zeke. Her brown eyes sparkled. "I sort of expected that you'd want to keep me naked."

"Very cool," said Zeke.

"Well, clothes are overrated," she added, casually.

The drive back to Marie Island was pleasant, and they dropped the windows and let the warm Florida breeze flow through the car. Tracy seemed languid and content.

"Good to be someplace warm," she said.

As soon as they'd arrived at the cottage, Tracy had changed into a dark green bikini accented with a large straw hat and matching straw sandals. Her beach cover-up was white and very short, showing off her shapely, toned legs. *She looks fabulous,* Zeke thought.

"I'm ready," she said. "Are we heading for the beach now?" She smelled like tanning oil and coconut.

As they walked to the beach Zeke asked, "How long do you have?"

"To visit?" she said. "I'm off all week."

"Return flight next Sunday?" Zeke calculated.

"Yep," she said. They found a spot in the sand a dozen feet from the water and put down their bag and small cooler. Zeke sat. Tracy took a deep breath.

"Gotta love the negative ions from the ocean, right?" she continued as she tossed down a towel and sat down near him. "That's actually what makes people feel so good at the beach."

"Really?" asked Zeke. "That's it, huh?" He smiled at her.

"Yep. Want a beer?" Tracy opened the cooler and handed Zeke a cold beer.

"Nice, thanks," he said. "Nice way to spend a week," he said.

"Indeed," she said.

"Who's watching your Labra doodle?" he asked innocently.

Tracy looked at him with no expression.

"Joking," said Zeke. "You work out mornings?"

"Yes. But not too early," she said. "I am on vacation."

"And do you want to show me your tattoo again?" he asked.

"Yep, sure do."

"Hmm," he thought out loud. "This may be the beginning of something beautiful."

ABOUT THE AUTHOR

Jeff Siebold loves a good mystery. A life long reader, he has embarked on a personal journey in creativity designed to contribute to the delight of mystery readers everywhere.

Jeff and his wife Karin live on a barrier island in North Carolina, not far from the Cape Fear River (made famous by one of his favorite authors, John D. MacDonald). They have three college-aged children and two unruly dogs.

Made in the USA
Charleston, SC
28 November 2016